We hope you enjoy this book.
Please return or renew it by the due date.
You can renew it at **www.norfolk.gov.uk/libraries**
or by using our free library app. Otherwise you can
phone **0344 800 8020** - please have your library
card and pin ready.
You can sign up for email reminders too.

NORFOLK COUNTY COUNCIL
LIBRARY AND INFORMATION SERVICE

NORFOLK ITEM

3 0129 08248 6862

THE GIRL SAVAGE

Katherine Rundell was born in 1987 and grew up in London, Southern Africa and Brussels. In 2008 she was elected a Fellow of All Souls College, Oxford. This is her first book and it was born of her love of Zimbabwe and her own childhood there. Her second book, *Rooftoppers*, was inspired by summers working in Paris and by night-time trespassing on the rooftops of Oxford Colleges, and has won and been shortlisted for numerous major prizes.

THE
GIRL
SAVAGE

Katherine Rundell

ff

faber and faber

First published in 2011
by Faber and Faber Limited
Bloomsbury House, 74–77
Great Russell Street, London WCIB 3DA

Typeset by Faber and Faber
Printed and bound by CPI Group (UK) Ltd, Croydon, CRO 4YY

A CIP record for this book
is available from the British Library

ISBN 978-0-571-25431-6

FSC
www.fsc.org
MIX
Paper from
responsible sources
FSC® C020471

To my parents

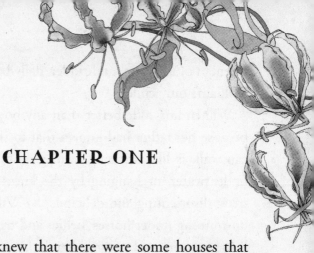

CHAPTER ONE

Wilhelmina knew that there were some houses that had glass in every window, and locks on the doors.

The farmhouse in which she lived was not one of them. If there was a key to the front door, Wilhelmina had never seen it: it was likely that the goats that wandered in and out of the kitchen had eaten it. The house was at the end of the longest of the farm roads, in the hottest corner of Zimbabwe. Her bedroom window was a square space in the wall. During the rains, she sewed plastic bags into a screen and stretched them across the frame. During the heat, the dust blew in.

Years ago, a visitor to the farm had asked Will about her window.

'Surely your father can afford a pane of glass?'

'I like to be dusty,' she had said, 'and wet.' Dust and rain made mud. Mud was full of possibilities.

The farm roads were bald and red with the settled dust. They were walked daily by Captain Browne, owner of the farm, driven daily by William Silver, foreman of the farm, and ridden daily by Wilhelmina, William's only child.

Wilhelmina rode better than any boy on the farm, because her father had known that to ride before you can walk is like drinking from glass bottles of Coke under water, or hanging by the knees from baobab trees: disorienting and delicious. So Wilhelmina grew up running under horses' bellies and tripping up into horse manure and tugging handfuls of her long dark hair when horseflies stung. The horseboys living in the tin-roofed cottages in the staff quarters never wept at horseflies – sometimes they swore in a leisurely, laughing way in Shona – *ach, booraguma* – and Wilhelmina was sure that she was the equal of any boy. She was faster than most of the boys her age on foot, too. And she was many other things; when the men on the farm talked her over in the evenings, they needed handfuls of *ands* to describe her: Will was stubborn, *sha*, and exasperating and wild and honest and true.

In the morning light of late October, Will was crouched on the floor stirring a pot of methylated spirit and water. Meths, applied to the feet, hardened the soles and made living shoes. There were six assorted chairs in the airy sitting room, but Will liked the floor. There was more space. Will had widely spaced eyes, and widely spaced toes, and was altogether a favourite of space. Her talk was spaced too, she knew; the slow talk of the African afternoon, with good gaps of silence.

Will heard the clatter of hooves, and a hungry whinnying. That meant William Silver was home from his early-morning gallop over the farm. Everyone in that part of Zimbabwe rose early. The main part of the day's work had to be done by lunch; and October was the hottest month. It melted the roads into tarred soup; birds got stuck in it.

The sitting room door opened, and a hairy face peered round it. Will felt the door open before she saw it; it was joy; Dad was back; she jumped up in one single movement, all speed and legs, and hurled herself into his arms, wrapping her feet around his waist. '*Dad!*'

'Morning! Morning, Wildcat.'

Will buried her face in her father's neck. 'Morning, Dad', she said, muffled. With most men, Will was tense-muscled: they left her half-marvelling and half-wary, and she made sure to keep her few steps of distance. She hated having to shake hands with the unknown skin of strangers; but Dad, with his muscled softness, was different.

'But I thought you were gone for the day, hey?' said William.

'Ja. Ja, soon. But I wanted to see your face first, Dad.

I missed you.' Will had been out at the tree house last night, asleep in the largeness of the night air by the time her father had got home. They could go for days without seeing each other, but she thought it made the happiness, when they did, sharper: more tangy. 'But now –' she scrambled up – 'now I can go, ja. I haven't fed Shumba, and Simon'll be waiting.' She turned at the door, wanting to say something that would mean, I love you. Goodness-how-I-do-love-you.

'*Faranuka*, Dad!' *Faranuka*. Will's Shona was good: and *Faranuka* was Shona for *be happy*.

Simon *was* waiting. Simon was Will's best friend. He was everything that she wasn't: a tall, fluid black boy to her waiflike, angular white girl. It had not been love at first sight. When Simon had arrived to train as a farm-hand, Will took one single look and with six-year-old certainty, announced that, *no*, she did not like him: he was *flimsy*. That was because Simon had enormous bushbaby eyes, tender trusting pools which seemed to hold tears, just ready to fall from beneath stupidly curled lashes.

But it didn't take long for Will to see that Simon was breathing, leaping, brilliant, proof that appearances are deceptive. In fact, she knew now, Si was a stretched-catapult of a boy, the scourge of the stables, with a hoarse laugh much too deep for him, and arms and legs that jerked and broke any passing cup or plate. His dislike of the tin bathtub, and his revelling in the softly squelching Zimbabwean mud meant that Simon had a distinctive smell. He smelt to the young Will of dust and sap and salt beef.

Will had smelt to Simon of earth and sap and mint.

So with such essential aspects in common – the sap, most obviously, but also the large eyes and the haphazard limbs – it was inevitable that the two fell in sort-of-love by the time they were seven, and by double figures they were friends of the firmest, most sticky and eternal sort.

Simon was the one who had taught Will how to bring her horse to a gallop on the home stretch to the stables, yelling 'Yah! Ee-yah! Come *on*, slowcoach!' And he taught her how to swing herself round to the underside of the neck and ride upside-down so that her long hair was coated with the flying dust, and her cheeks slipped into her eyes.

They swapped languages. He learnt her Zimbabwean-twanged English and she – with tongue-poked-out concentration – the basics of his Chikorekore Shona. She showed him how to swim under water for minutes at a time. The trick was to breathe in slowly: not a gulp, but patiently and through pursed lips, like sucking a straw. Her feet became dark brown and hardened from years of barefoot races across the fields, and her nails were filthy.

Since last December, Simon had lived with his brother Tedias in the staff quarters, a block of brick huts and fires on the edge of Two Tree Hill Farm. The name, Captain Browne had said, rolling one of his cigarettes in tobacco-green fingers, was a kind of bad joke, because there were several hundred trees on Two Tree Hill, enough to obliterate the hill itself. In fact, he said, it would have been better named Just Tree Farm. Or Tree Tree Tree Tree Tree Farm. Ha ha, Captain Browne.

But of course there were clear patches, made of brown grass and shimmering heat and anthills and it was across one of these that Will now ran, kicking the backs of her feet against her bottom and singing. As soon as she was within shouting distance of Simon's mudbricked home, Will gave her best Shona call.

'*Ee-weh!*' Shouting distance on that farm was at least a field-length further than anywhere else, because the air was still and there were no cars except for the truck; a little noise went a gloriously long way. 'Simon! Simon! You in, Si?'

Simon picked his nose in a pointed sort of way. He was squatting outside the hut just within the shade of the brown thatch roof, drinking Coke from a glass bottle. Tedias nudged Simon with his toe. He spoke in Shona, '*Uchaenda*. Up, boy. Off with you to the little madam.'

The 'little madam' was an old joke. The shrill and imperious 'madam' of the typical farmer's wife couldn't be further from Will's brown and gold manners.

Simon threw an aggrieved pebble at Will's feet. '*Will*.' He scowled. 'Where you *been*? I thought you weren't coming. You such a slowcoach, man.' She wasn't, but he said it anyway. 'Like a caterpillar with no legs. Was going to go off without you just now, madman.' '*Madman*' was Simon's variation on madam. They both thought it was closer to the truth.

'Oh, sorry; *sorry*, Si, truly. Sorry-sorry.' Will didn't give explanations.

She stared up at Tedias – whom Will loved achingly: he was a hero, big and scarred and restfully silent. She had to squint because the sun was strong now, beating in the edgeless blue of the sky.

'*Mangwanani*, Tedias.' She bobbed the curtsey she gave to the Captain's visitors. *Mangwanani*, which meant good morning. Her Simon did not need to be saluted, but Tedias, in his slow largeness, his bare chest and his kindness to the dogs, deserved respect.

'*Mangwanani*, Will.' He pronounced her name like all the men on the farm, *wheel*, and her father had picked it up, called her Buck and Wheel, Cartwheel,

Catherine Wheel. '*Marara sei*, Wheel? Did you sleep?'

There was a formal answer to that, but Will, to her annoyance, found she'd forgotten it. There were codes in Shona she hadn't yet learnt, and she quivered now; there was so much to know, there were subtleties that hung out of sight, things that she knew she didn't know she didn't know. She said, '*Ndarara…ah…ndarara kana mararawo.*' I slept well if you slept well.

Tedias nodded with what seemed to be approval (though you couldn't be sure with other people, Will thought, staring up at his slow, heavy smile: that was a central rule to life, the one thing you *could* be sure of.) '*Ndarara*, Will, yes', said Tedias. 'I slept.'

Simon, Will could see, was growing tired of the formalities. He finished his Coke, burped, wiped his mouth with the back of his hand, and threw down the bottle. He dribbled with it, out along the path. 'Come *on*, Will. Mad-man mad-cat Will.' He hopped backwards, so that each hop landed on *on*, 'come-on-come-on-come-*on*, girl.'

But Will stayed in the sun, trying not to smile. Because Will didn't take orders from anyone. She crouched down, making her most aggravating proud-face, and began scratching a W in the dirt with a long stick. A beetle lumbered up it, on to her arm and she stilled herself, enjoying the tickling feeling of its thread-thin feet. It was deep green with shimmers of blue and turquoise and pitch-black legs. She kissed it very softly. If happiness were a colour, it would be the colour of this beetle, thought Will.

There was a whistle. Will grinned: Simon's whistles were so perfect that they could speak whole archways of emotion: shock, happiness, hot admiration, look out!: this one said, 'I'm waiting.' With maybe a hint of: 'and I'm hungry'. They were planning a quick raid on the mango tree and a picnic by the rock pool: she should go, she knew.

But it was hard for Will Silver to keep firm hands on herself, because small things – dragonflies, earwigs, sticks with peeling bark, warm rain, those wonderful curls of fur behind the dogs' ears – they had a strange way of making time disappear. She had wondered, often, if other people felt the same way, but had never been able to explain it properly; that feeling of sharpness and fullness.

Simon whistled again. He meant it this time, Will could tell. She jumped up to standing, whipped up an imaginary horse – whooping her throaty, 'Yagh! Yah!' – and tore past him. Will was fast, and proud of it. She ran tilting forward, dark skin stark against the white-blue of the sky and the yellow-green of the grass. 'Race you, Si!' she called: but she didn't say where to.

Simon hurtled after her. She was uncatchable in this mood, like a bushfire, infectious and exasperating at

9

once. She might run for miles and miles and miles.

As he threw his long legs after her, he cried, 'Look at the little madman! Look at that dirt! *Ach*, pity our poor foreman – his little girl's gone wild!'

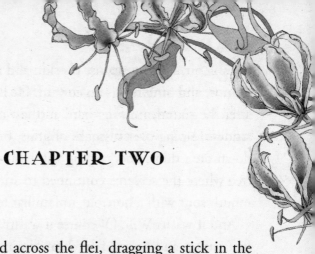

CHAPTER TWO

Simon walked across the flei, dragging a stick in the dust. Will had disappeared yesterday without a word; in the middle of a particularly good race on horseback she had just swerved away, over a stack of firewood and off. It was one of the hazards of being her friend, that you might be left for hours, days – even, once, a week – waiting for her to return, while she rambled over the bush, singing softly, eating fruit, telling stories to aloes and birds. She was a funny one, and there was nothing you could do about it. But he was bored, *so bored*: practising round-offs was no fun without her, nor was tracking the men working in the fields; and there was nobody to steal bananas from the kitchen garden. Simon kicked at a dung beetle in the path. He sighed, and kicked, and sighed again.

And then the day tore open. A scream shrieked across the flei; there was a shattering, clattering cacophony of fear as birds took off from the trees. It came again; it was a shriek of inhuman agony, hammering against the still air, beating against his skin and raising goose-bumps, and Simon was no coward. He hurled himself after the sound, running hard and fast and with long strides, leaping over tussocks of grass, bringing a foot down on a thorn and gasping with pain, reaching the tree where the screams continued to sting the air, his mouth sour with a horrible, unfamiliar fear –

And it wasn't Will. Of course it wasn't. That was the first thing; and as relief hit him Simon doubled up, clutching a stitch, retching. It was a group of boys and they were holding – not just holding; he retched again, this time in disgust – torturing a monkey, pulling at the arms, snatching out the legs into an agonising straight line, snuffling with snot-bubbling amusement.

This was absolute cruelty. And Simon hadn't known Will for all those years for nothing: he knew how to deal with absolutes. He tightened his body into hard readiness; balled his hands, clenched his toes, locked his elbows, but when he spoke, it was softly; 'What – d'you think – you're – doing?'

The boys paused, alarmed by the sudden boy with his lips folded back in a snarl.

'Stop it! Stop it *now*.' His voice was steady. He raised one fist. '*Now*.'

The tallest of the group, who was wearing lace-up shoes and so was probably a rich city boy, shifted awkwardly.

'We're just playing, ja?' He sneered, sizing up his

tall, thin, dusty opponent, 'And actually it's none of your blerry business, farm boy.'

'No. *No, actually*, you wrong.' Simon flared his nostrils. 'It *is* my business, *city boy*.' They stared at each other, both ugly with dislike and working themselves into heavy, rhythmical breathing. 'But if I'm just a farm boy – and just so's you know, I'm a *horse*boy, actually, ja, I look after Mr Browne's stable – then you won't be afraid to fight, *ja*?' Simon's skin felt stretched with his anger. The boy was a good year or two older than he was and built like a boxer, stocky with fat and muscle. Now the boy hissed, half in fear and half in exasperation, and he thrust the monkey into the hands of the boy behind him, where it struggled, shrieking a high cry of terror.

'*Stupid*. You're *stupid*. *Penga*. Stupid *horseboy*. I promise you, hey, you do *not* want to fight me.'

'No, *actually*. I do.'

'Ja?'

'Ja, *actually*.'

Simon leapt and at the same moment the boy leapt and they thudded together in mid-air, but the boy was heftier, and grunting, he knocked against Simon's chest and pinned him to the hot earth, rolling his face in the dust. He snatched back the monkey and held it tauntingly, over Simon's face. 'So come get it, *horseboy*.'

There was a crashing of undergrowth, a rearing horse, and a choked cry –

'I saw you, hey – you're *foul*.'

A thumping of feet as a body dropped to the ground –

'Foul! I saw you! How *dare* you?'

A small brown fist connected with the boy's triumphant cheek, and a brown foot knocked the legs from under his solid torso.

'*Foul!* You're *foul*.'

The boy looked up. Standing over him, looking down and vibrating with rage, was a small white girl, with a large mouth and heavy eyebrows and brown eyes flecked with anger. She held the monkey, clutched with one hand to her chest.

'I won't kick you.' The voice was strangled, shrill, jagged with anger. 'I don't kick dogs. So I won't kick you.' Will drew breath. She could face irate horses, and knew what to do with snakes, rats and baboons. Humans were more difficult. '– But you can't do that.' Will swore. 'You can't just *tear stuff apart*, right? You *foul* . . .' She felt angrier than she'd ever been, and she was sweaty and drawing breath was a struggle, but she gasped, 'the monkeys . . . you *dare* . . . they're good and they're fragile and they're *golden*.'

'*Golden*?' Even lying in the dirt, the boy managed to look incredulous.

'Yeah. *Golden. Precious*. You . . . you're . . .' Will found she had no words, so she hocked back her chin and spat, accurately, on the boy's forehead. 'Unlike *you*.'

14

And Will was up on Shumba again, bareback. In a few moments, she would feel properly victorious. For now, she only wanted to cry. The monkey was whining in her lap, so she licked a finger and stroked down the disordered fur. It was beautiful: grey and velvety-soft. She said, 'Si? You coming, hey?'

'Ja. In a minute,' said Simon. 'You go on. Meet at the tree house, 'kay?'

Shumba was hard to wheel around without reins, and it would be so bathetic and terrible to fall off now, so Will thundered on in a straight line. She was going the wrong way for home, which was foolish; but now that the boy was down and the monkey was safe and held with one hand inside her shirt her anger was trickling out of her. It went so slowly that she could feel it. It was, she thought, like having had cement in her veins; but now the blood was coming back.

The monkey chattered, and scratched against her skin. She whispered to it, just soft noises at first (because, what did you say to a frightened monkey?) and then when it still cried, Will whispered, 'hush, monkey: hush, beauty: hush, dear heart', and it grew quiet, lulled by the rocking of her steady riding. Will was free to listen to the beat of the horse's feet and the swish-*swish*, swish-*swish* of the three-foot grass. The grass in Africa speaks, and now, she thought, it sang to her, 'hush, beauty: hush, beauty'. And scratches and bruises could be dealt with later: for now, she was victorious and alone, and there would be ice-cold chocolate pudding at lunch, and she had the solid warmth of horse and a baby monkey, and the road was pure sunlight.

Simon stood watching Will's galloping back and then turned, awkwardly, to the boy, who still lay on the ground. He held out a hand.

'Peace, hey?'

A pause. Then, without a smile, the boy nodded. 'Peace.'

'Here. Give me your hand.' Simon hauled him up. They stood, face to face. Simon scratched at a scab on his chin. The boy picked his teeth and rolled the result between finger and thumb.

'We *were* just playing', he said.

Silence.

'I could have beaten her, hey? But I wouldn't fight a girl. But,' in grudging admiration, 'we'll leave the 'boons alone now.'

Simon grinned. 'You couldn't beat her. She's a crazy, that one. And strong like a 'pard.'

The boy snorted and flicked his now-circular toothpickings into a thorn tree.

'Ja. But she's still just a girl.'

'Nah, man. She's different, right? Like fire. She's a wildcat girl.'

CHAPTER THREE

Will was good at lighting fires. She was proud of it. Because fire was such an odd thing – it was like water, she reckoned; if we didn't have the name for it, didn't have it every day, we'd be so choked and laughing and flabbergasted by it. Will tried to teach Simon this strange-wonder, but it wasn't really a success.

'No, but *look*. Look properly.' She blew on the flames, and she jabbed Simon with a twig. '*Look*, Si. Like it's alive and it's also-not-really-alive. Watch: it moves without wind. D'you see?' She blew harder, and sparks shot into the air. 'It *is* amazing, isn't it, Si?'

'Ja. I guess. It is. ' Simon looked unconvinced. He wished it would heat up faster. They had lit the fire at the foot of the tree house, which meant there was no breeze to help it along but had the great advantage that they knew they couldn't be disturbed. When they were younger, they had done their cooking in the bread-smelling kitchen, but then the two of them had set fire to the wall (Simon said it was Will's fault: Will said it was both of them) frying bantam eggs in oil that was too spitting-hot. The wall was still stained black, and Will still made her ashamed-smiling face whenever she passed it.

Since then, Will had had to bake her food in open fires, or in the hollows of the tree roots, which was nicer anyway; she could make meals that tasted enticingly of smoke and leaves, and eggs and animal, and Africa.

Simon stretched, and snuffed at the smoke. 'It's ready now, ja.'

'You've got no patience, Si,' said Will; and that was rich, thought Simon, because she had even less. 'It needs more wood, hey, it's still hungry.'

'Ja. But more's to the point, *I'm* still hungry. It *is* ready. 'Ts just you're blind like a chungololo . . . *Ow!*'

Will had picked up a gooseberry from the pile at her side and flicked it at Simon's head.

'Hey! That's my eye, mad girl'. He flicked one back from his own pile and Will caught it in her mouth – 'ha-*ha!*' – and inside she burned and whooped with pleasure. *That* was how life should be: snap-gulp-whoop. She grinned, with yellow gooseberry seeds between her teeth. 'Ja, OK. You win. Fire's ready.'

Together they split open the banana skins with shards of sharp flint. Kezia chattered and tugged at the bunch in Will's hand. After only a week, Will had trained her to sleep inside her shirt, and to sit on her shoulder and chew at her hair. The bananas today were the best on the farm, in celebration of Kezia's cleverness.

Simon sprinkled salt and pepper on to the green ones, and used a single wet finger to poke brown sugar into the yellow. Will was emptying her pockets, looking for a fatly folded envelope she had put there this morning. Elastic for her hair, a mint, a ball of dog hair and dust, a masasa pod, a catapult, more unidentifiable animal hair, a now-wilted jacaranda flower –

'There! That's for you, Si.'

She watched anxiously as Simon peered inside the envelope; there was large slice of good white bread and two squares of mint chocolate. The envelope was a big one that had held legal-looking letters, but Will judged it had served its purpose, and she had borne it away in triumph. Captain Browne was in fact this moment searching furiously for it, but it hadn't occurred to her to ask permission: paper was not a 'permission' thing. The only things she could not take were money – and what would she do with that, here, in the sun? – or grain from the planting bins, or water belonging to the men in the compound, which she would have been honestly ashamed to do. Beyond that, Will was free.

Simon's eyes glinted, 'Excellent! Chocolate. Ach, Ndatenda hangu! I love mint.'

Pulling a leaf from a branch that poked inquisitively over his shoulder, Simon laid it out like a plate.

'Budge up, Wildcat, ja. You're in my way.'

'I can't! Your big feet are taking up my space.'

'*My* feet! Yours're bigger.'

It was true. Will grinned. Her feet were enormous. She shuffled sideways as, biting his tongue with concentration, Simon crushed the chocolate into powder and sprinkled it on the bananas.

'There. Looks good, hey, Will?'

It looked almost unbearably delicious: sugar-brown against chocolate-brown against soft, fibrous banana-yellow. Will's mouth was tingling, and she wrapped foil round the fruit as Simon handed them to her with greedy, stomach-quivering quickness. Her fingers were long and brown and out of proportion, people said, to the smallness of the rest of her.

'Done!'

Simon nodded approval. 'Ja. You want to put them in?'

Putting bananas into the embers was a minor act of bravery and therefore something to be fought over.

'Together,' said Will. 'On three, OK?'

'OK. And no cheating, hey, Will? Ja? OK? No cheating? On three. One . . .' Simon was licking his hands to protect against fire.

'Two . . .'

They both cheated and went on two. They always did. Laughing and together they pushed the foil packages deep into the papery embers of the fire. Will snatched back cooked fingers and bit her lip to stop herself wincing. Simon made a meal of his small burn, hamming it up, sucking his teeth – '*Ona*! Look! *Aish*! Ow, Will,' – but Will only laughed; Simon was like that; sympathy only made him worse. She held herself still. The best bit, really, was this: the waiting with her chin on her knees while the bananas made promising noises. It was a fat, luscious feeling.

They split the bit of bread, straight and fair down the middle. Simon nudged Will with his toe.

'You got more than me.' He reached his long arm across to grab Will's piece.

Will snatched it away, held it safe behind her back. She widened her eyes in mock anger. 'I do not!'

'Do.'

'Do not!' This was a ritual, familiar to Will as food itself.

'Do!'

'*Not!*' They launched themselves at each other, Will trying to pull Simon's nose, ears. Simon had the advantage; he could grab handfuls of her hair, and she wondered in a breathless way about cutting it, as she ducked and kicked, and tried to bite at Simon's ankle; it would make fighting easier.

Captain Browne, watching them, had once compared them to his scrapping terriers; but that wasn't quite right. They were different, swifter and lighter; young leopards would have been more appropriate.

Will had Simon down and knelt on his chest.

'OK, OK.' Simon panted '*Do not*. Get off me, you madman. You're like a pregnant hippo.'

'Good.' Will lay back, red-faced but victorious, shimmeringly happy, and stared at the sky. 'I'll swap, Si, if you want.'

'Nah. Actually – 'Simon's smile was wicked, thought Will, *wicked*, and her nose prickled with affection – 'I think mine's bigger,' and without scraping off the earth it had gathered he crammed the entire piece into his mouth.

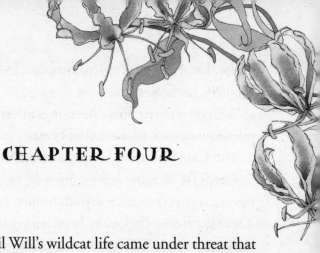

CHAPTER FOUR

It wasn't until Will's wildcat life came under threat that she realised how dearly she loved it.

It began three days after the tree-house fire, with a convoy of cars drawing up in the courtyard. This was unheard-of: nobody visited the Captain. He was known, they said, to like his privacy, up there behind his crumbling old walls. And his mongrels farted at the tea table. And yet now five farmers were clambering out of five cars, kicking at the dogs that swarmed round their legs. They explained their mission.

Captain Browne, grimly entertained, rang the cowbell. It had 'Staff' engraved in bronze.

'Yes, boss?' Lazarus appeared, barefoot. His shirt was buttoned awry; all the men, including William Silver, worked bare-chested when nobody was around.

'Ah, Lazarus.' Captain Browne felt surreptitiously for his handkerchief. He used the cowbell only when other farmers were present, and a year's worth of dust had transferred itself to his hands. 'Yes. Fetch Will, please, Lazarus.' And, as Lazarus hesitated, '*Both* Wills. Quickly, Lazarus, man.'

William arrived first, hurrying in with a politely questioning look and a tray of beers.

The Captain smiled under cover of his moustache. 'It seems, Will, that your young wildcat has been trespassing on every farm within twenty miles of here. These gentlemen feel we've been letting her run wild.'

'Trespassing?' William bit the inside of his cheeks to hold back the smile. 'I see. We'll have to talk to Will about that. She should be here any minute . . .' The men stood in an awkward semicircle, holding drinks and sucking their teeth, until there was the crash of a door, running footsteps and Will was with them, launching herself at her father to kiss his rough face – and freezing abruptly, one leg off the ground, at the sight of strangers.

They were sunburnt, thick necked, pot-bellied men, hoarse and coarse with fat fingers. Harsh but fair, they said. Sometimes just harsh. One of them – the fattest, who wore, of all things, a Rolex watch – held two children by the hand. Will could feel them all staring at her; at her cut-off jeans, marked at the back where she had been sitting in the grass; at the long scar across her knee, where she had fallen from a tree on to an acacia bush; at her long feet and fingers and long eyebrows and long mouth. She stared at the floor.

'So *this* is Lilibet's girl, William?' The fat man's voice was low and rough. All tobacco farmers sounded the same: it was the sound of fifty cigarettes a day. Ochre-coloured voices, William called them. 'She's the spitting image of her mother. Aren't you, Wilhelmina?'

'Oh.' Will said. 'Um.' She tried again. 'Ja – I –'

It was the best she could do, first because she had more of a loosely sketched idea of her mother than a proper memory; and second, because there were no mirrors in the farm. And she didn't want to say anything anyway; she stood motionless, breathing hard. She *wished* she hadn't come in, had stayed outside with Simon and Peter; she could have been playing stuck-in-the-mud-in-the-trees, or their improvised version of polo, with pilfered brooms and unripe lemons she tugged off the lemon tree with her teeth. But there was nothing for it now –

The man was raising his eyebrows. 'Like I was saying, Charles. William. She can't stay here. I will *not* suffer trespassing, William. And – more important, ja – the girl needs her own kind.' This was white farmer's code: *white girls need white girls.*

'What?' Will's frown burrowed her forehead deep into her nose. Oh, *what*? That was ignorance; that was the sort of pre-packaged idea that didn't belong in her farm, her world. She struggled to be polite, but she was angry. 'I think I'm fine like this, actually, thank you, sir. Truly, truly, actually, fine.' She couldn't hold back a spray of spit with the last word, '*Fine.*' The men stepped back, wiping their faces.

With an obvious effort, they smiled. They were wearing awkward, oh-what-a-sweet-little-girl faces; and they looked, she thought, *ridiculous*. The speaker – who was Adam Madison, the biggest landowner this side of Mutare – looking rather grieved.

'Ja, my dear, I'm sure you think that's true, hey.' And he went on, speaking over her head, which she hated, 'But look at the girl, William. She hasn't got any of the things females need, man. She hasn't got – '

And although Will knew that Zimbabwean girls never, never interrupted their seniors, she couldn't help bursting out here, frowning but relieved, because if that was the problem then she had conclusive proof –

'That's not *true* – I've got *everything*. Sir. I've got more than everything. Don't I, Dad? I've got ten bantams that lay eggs all over the house, and I've got the boys – Simon and Peter, and there's Penga and Learnmore – but especially Simon – and I've got Kezia, my monkey – and Shumba, that's my horse – and I've got more fruit than we could ever eat, and I've got books, and paints and the Captain said I can paint my ceiling with birds if I can find a ladder, and I've got my own mango tree, called Marmaduke, and I've got . . .' this was a sworn secret between her and Simon, but it came burbling out, 'I've got a nest of three baby hyrax – rock-rabbits, ja? – in the barn, and I'm going to feed them on currants and *naajies* and *sadza* and train them to sit on my shoulders.' And Will felt suddenly brown and strong in victory, because when all was said, nobody could argue with a world like hers.

William looked down at his daughter. He appeared to be trying not to laugh. His eyes travelled from the two children clinging to the farmer's sleeve to the four-foot-six of vibrating brown skin next to him. *She needs her own kind.* Madison's girl was dressed in a spotless white tennis dress and patent-leather shoes, and, he thought, she had a very patent-leather sort of face to match. Beneath the curls, she was rather ordinary-looking. The boy, about two years older, was making faces at his reflection in the window, straightening his hair. Next to them, his wild Will looked grubby and torn, and that scratch on her leg needed some antiseptic. Her large mouth, set against the fragility of her jaw, made her look unbalanced. William thought her absolutely, irrefutably the most beautiful creature living, the most beautiful that would ever live: but she was certainly of a different species from the farmer's pink-and-white princess.

Apparently the other men had been having much the same thoughts, because there was a sudden burst of hearty, raucous laughter.

'Nah, William! You're right!' Although he had not spoken.

'Ach. Let her be.'

'Leave that one to the horseboys.'

'Ja, no!' And Madison nearly choked on his own hefty amusement. 'Keep her off my land if you can, or I'll wallop her. But you're right. That one would take a lot of house-breaking.'

Soon after that day, there came the monthly gala-doings on the farm, in which every man down-tooled and lit fires by the cottages, and there was acrobatics and dancing in traditional dress, and women and whooping and roasted meat. And Will's skin-of-her-teeth escape from the farmers meant she had something real and important to celebrate. She rose early, while it was still dark, and swung out of bed without bothering to change out of her pyjamas. She crept out of the house by the front door (the back door squeaked) and ran, light-footed, to fetch Shumba and to waken the sleeping horseboys. The festival meant that the fields would be empty; miles and miles of open ground.

'Simon. *Simon*! Peter! Wake up! It's here. It's today! Wake *up*, Si.' She crept over to the mattress on the floor and put her hand over his nose.

Simon choked and awoke, kicking and gasping.

'*Ach*! Don't *do* that, mad girl.' Then, as the dawn

light struggled into the room, 'Is it today, Will?'

'Yes! Today! Today, *today*!' Today there would be un-limited time, unlimited sun, unlimited food. Will leapt into the air, seized her ankles, somersaulted. '*Today*!'

On days like these, when the fields were silent and the horses needed little guiding, they could trespass wherever they pleased, jumping over billycans of water and stone walls.

Will rode ahead on the broad back of her own brown Shumba, calling back, '*Faga moto*, boys!' Which meant, *make fire*, let's go, move faster. She could feel her lungs in her chest – beating-beating-beating in time with her heart – and she was suddenly giddy, drunk with the day, high-pitched in hilarity. '*Faga-faga-mo TO*!'

Simon kicked his horse into a burst of speed – 'Ja, *faga moto* yourself, girl!' – and they raced, too fast for safety, but never quite fast enough, across the flei.

'Faster! Come on, Shumba, faster!' Will shook the sweat out of her eyes. It was impossible to be sweet and humble when the wind whistled like this through her ears. 'Come on, Peter! Come on, Si! Calypso'll go faster'n *that*.'

Will dropped her reins: she couldn't, couldn't stay calm under that mad-chaos of speed and sun, she was wild to show off, and she rose with deliberate wobbles to stand on Shumba's wide back. With her gums ex-posed to the early morning air, she whooped and gave the horseboy's call, 'Ai-ai-aiyah!', and Simon, a length behind, called back – 'ai-ai-*aiya!*'

Peter, a nervous hump on the brown nag, blind to the thundering beauty of the day, pulled his mouth down into his chin in panic; 'Look *out*, you idiot!' Will wobbled again – not on purpose this time – and laughed, 'I am, Peter, I *am*. Oh Peter, I know you're an angel but you're a fool, Pete. Look!'

Intoxicated with her success and his awed eyes, and with the way the wind rushed by and flicked delicate strands of saliva across her cheeks, Will spread out her arms, spun in a pirouette. Shumba chose that moment to stumble over a rabbit hole and with a terrific crash, that sounded and resounded for miles and miles of flei, Will fell into the long grass.

'Woah!' Simon pulled to a halt, tugging at Calypso's mane, dragging him round, tense with shock. 'Will? *Will?*'

Peter had been unable to stop, fumbling with reins and nearly tipping over the neck of the nag; now he trotted back, and the two boys waited, uncertain what was needed – laughter or bandages? –

'Will? You OK?'

'All well, Will? Will . . . ?'

There was a pause, with only muffled gasps and expletives from the grass – but Will was a *fighter*; she was proud of that, a fighter, and she worked out which way was up in the mass of green and stood, shaking and covered in grass-seeds.

'Ja.' she panted. 'Of course I am. 'Course!'

In fact she wasn't sure what was happening in her chest, and her elbow was grazed and bleeding and she was only half-breathing, and half-crying and half-laughing: but she seized Shumba's mane, and swung up again, scrabbling against his sturdy sides, and ran a tongue over her teeth – 'All well! Ja! All all all well!' – and, lying low on Shumba's neck, Will galloped, still dizzy, out into the bush.

The boys, racing after her, heard singing on the wind.

When Will sang, she smiled at the same time; the corners of her mouth reached outwards, into her ears, and her eyes changed colour, to amber with bits of gold. This was Will's world, and it was her joy.

CHAPTER FIVE

If you wanted to see Will's world at its best, you went out at sunset. You had to put up with the swarms of mosquitoes, that was true, but in return you got the toads singing, and the air tasted of excitement. The African witching hour, the men called it. And it was true, Will thought, looking round at the circle of horseboys and the cobs of roast corn scattered on the ground; everything was strange in this light. Even the men drinking leftover beer from the gala two days before looked stronger and wilder than usual. It was like the world was carved out of expectant silence. Will sniffed and tucked her legs under her chin. Her knees smelt the same as the air; of woodsmoke and earth. Had anyone ever been as happy as her?

Her thoughts were interrupted by a colossal crash. It was Simon, back late from mucking the horses, pushing through the other boys, tripping and swearing, throwing a stick at someone's head, stealing someone else's corncob and collapsing to sit beside

Will. She grinned. Simon had never done anything quietly in his life.

'*Manheru*, hey!' He took a handful of the gooseberries by her side and crammed them into his mouth.

'*Manheru*!' Will leaned towards him. 'Hold still.'

'What?'

'Tick.' She pulled at the black insect on his arm and it came away, complete. 'You got to keep the head on – see, this one's good.' She held it out to Hector, who was two years younger and desperately in awe of her. 'If it stays in your skin, you're scuppered, ja. You froth at the mouth and die.' She smiled her most beatific smile. 'Truly.' She put the tick between her teeth and bit. Blood squeezed down her lips.

'Eugh! Will, that's horrible! Now you'll get rabies', warned Peter.

Will grinned at the expressions of horror on the boys' faces. She kissed the back of her hand and the blood on her lips left a lipstick-like-mark. 'It won't hurt me.'

Simon laughed. 'Nah, Will's immune to, like, *everything*.'

Will made her rabid-dog face. Hector rolled his eyes into his head and dribbled. 'I've got rabies! Look! *Look*, Will! I've got rabies too!'

Biting ticks was one of the very few things forbidden by Captain Browne.

'But they bit me first,' Will had said, trying to look sullen. 'And –' this was daring – 'I bet you bit ticks when you were a kid? Didn't you, sir?'

'Eh?' The Captain had growled low, like a lion with a blocked nose, and swiped at the back of her legs with his walking stick. 'Eh? Whatasay?' The Captain was deaf only when it was convenient. 'Run off and play with those boys of yours.' She had heard him snorting with laughter as he went round the corner. In fact, that had been the day she realised you could be as rude as you liked to the Captain – or you could be mute or say stupid things or be awkward and dirty and scratching – so long as you loved him at the same time. It was a thing worth knowing.

The other things that the Captain had forbidden were playing near the compost heap, where there were scorpions and some of the smaller snakes – which Will and Simon did anyway, and were duly bitten, but by a grass snake, no more dangerous than a wasp – and eating the dark red berries that grew along the veranda. Will only tried that once, and then never again, after the foulest fit of diarrhoea she had ever had. 'I thought I was going to die – but I would have hated to have died in a toilet. So I went out into the bush, ja, without any pants . . . and it was beautiful, and there were duiker by the stream, and it was so still . . . I think it was the beauty, ja, that cured me.' And above all, it was forbidden to wear clothes that had not been ironed; even vests; even *socks*. Ironing was the only way to kill the putsi fly that laid eggs on damp clothes and burrowed into your arms and legs without you feeling it.

Will had no real wish to have flies laying eggs under her skin, so the next afternoon she had dragged the heavy ironing board outside, bumped it against her shins, cursing, and up the steps, and out on to the veranda where she stood in the open air, ironing her father's socks.

She had already done all her own scraps of clothing; jeans bleached greyish-blue by the sun; T-shirts worn into flopping flapping softness; brightly patterned shorts which she made herself with clumsy stitches, and a khaki skirt she had made from the top of her father's trousers. There were dresses, too, that Captain Browne brought back as gifts from town. Most felt pointless in a house with no mirrors, and they were too tight, with bows that tangled at the back, but she could cut off the ribbons and use them to tie back her hair, and with one particularly fussy one she had sewn up the arms and neck and used it as a sack for stealing bananas.

Will should have worn a hat – children in Harare, she was told, wore wide-brimmed cloth or American-style caps – but the horseboys did not, and so Will did not. Nor did she wear socks herself; she didn't wear shoes; but her father did, and while Will rather liked the idea of trying putsi fly herself, she wouldn't have worms burrowing into her father's feet. She loved him too extremely. Though she couldn't have explained why, around him it was never difficult to keep her temper; around him there was never any need to tense up and contract into herself.

She could hear him now, coming in through the back door. It was in two parts, like a stable door, and the bottom half squeaked, but Will stubbornly refused to let anyone oil it, so that she would always be ready, like this, waiting on tiptoe to welcome her father. All the men who worked for Captain Browne – and in truth the Captain himself – were a little afraid of Will: so the door remained un-oiled.

She knew exactly what her father would do; this was the only bit of a day that never varied. Hot and tired (the tired that comes from a long day at a job at which he was *magnificent*, she thought, and felt a butterfly-flicker of happy pride), he would stride to the fridge, take out a glass bottle of beer, prise it open with his nails, and put his head under the single tap in the big tin sink.

'Hello? You in, Cartwheel?' he called.

He wasn't like other fathers, Will knew. He was taller and braver. She gave her owl hoot, loud as a shout, so

36

he would know she was by the avocado tree on the veranda. (A hoopoe call meant she was in her bedroom; and a parrot screech meant the rock pool.)

Her father always did everything hugely. With a lion's roar, he burst through the insect curtain and snatched Will up round the waist, and they spun and whirled, giddily out of balance and water droplets flew from William's face and the iron wobbled dangerously and the dogs barked, leaping and excited, and scratched at Will's spinning ankles, and William bellowed his great happy laugh – a laugh that only came out around Will, which she knew, and loved him even better for it – and hundreds of birds took off, chattering, from the avocado tree. Will glowed.

'Good day, hey, Dad?' she said when, set the right way up, she had picked up her iron from the floor.

'Good day. Long day . . . but good day.' He spoke in the way of the African evening, slowly, with long spaces. 'Lazarus said one of the goats had twins. One is too small . . . a runt. I said if he gave it to Tedias, Tedi would give it to you and you'd look after it. Ja?'

'*Ja*. Of course.' She looked at her father, and her slow, drunken-love smile, the one she reserved for him, took over her face. 'I'd love that, Dad. We could call it Nguruve, hey, to encourage it.'

Nguruve was Shona for pig: and Shumba was Shona for lion; and the Captain's terrier puppy was called

37

Bumhi, which was the fiercest kind of wild dog; and she was called wildcat. 'Everything has parts of other things,' she'd told Simon. She'd been trying to say, nobody is just sweet, or just cruel. Simon had said, 'Ja: you've got eyebrows like *chongololos*.' He had crocodile, she reckoned, and leopard, and horse in him.

As if he'd followed the last part of her thought, her father said, 'I found Simon upside-down on duty, hand-standing in the veggie patch. I hit him on the head with a cabbage.'

Will laughed. She could picture it.

'And Lucian Mazarotti's back from Harare.'

'Oh! Is he better?' Lucian had had cholera.

'Better. Healthy and strong as a lion. Strong as *you*, little Cartwheel. And he brought back six sacks of mealie porridge, and a drum of oil, and a bull calf for his heifer tied up in his truck like a chicken. Ja –' and her father's smile was slower than his speech, deep and satisfied –'all is well with him. He's got that gleam back on his skin: like a god.'

'Good! I'm glad. *Good!*' Will felt her stomach blaze with pleasure. Lucian owned the land on the outskirts of Two Tree Farm. He was Will's hero. There were diviners on the farm who could find boreholes with two sticks and a strange, inborn feeling for water: and Will reckoned Lucian was like that with people. It was as though he undug goodness from the hard unused centres of souls. He'd taught her to swim, and had held a large finger under her spine for her first back-bend, and had picked her up bodily when she fell off her horse, and he was generous with food. It was always Lucian who started off the singing when the men worked in the fields. 'That's good, Dad.' She would have said, 'send love for me', but Lucian would have been embarrassed.

'And . . . Cynthia Vincy drove by West Edge,' said William. 'Again.'

'Oh.' A syllable can express a great deal; Will's sounded of resignation; but also of swear words, and the smells of rotting vegetation, and wary amusement and bitten fingernails.

Captain Browne had met Cynthia Vincy on his last trip into Harare. She was a widow, much younger than the Captain and much, much better looking. She was not the typical farmer's wife, who were leather-skinned and masculine; Cynthia Vincy was well-dressed, strong-jawed, long-legged, conscious of her power over men: formidable.

Will had taken just one look and had known that the Captain – who was usually stern and a little for-bidding – was a goner: scribbled, head-over-heels, a smitten-kitten. And Cynthia Vincy must have known it, because now she often drove along the road that bordered the farm. She never stopped when Will's father was there because she'd taken a hissing dislike to his wary eyes and massive, rough frame, but when it was only the Captain and the men she would clamber out to ask his opinion on some problem, wriggling and cooing admiration. And, William said, she was false as plastic flowers, like air conditioning against honest wind, margarine against butter, false as *dammit*; 'She asks him about tobacco – simple things, storage, harvesting times; with big eyes; nodding with those open lips, ja – but she *knows* about tobacco. Her husband was a tobacco farmer, for *pity's sake*.'

Will had never seen Cynthia up close but that didn't stop her hating her, intensely and by instinct. Thinking about it, Will put down the iron and ran her fingers through her hair, gripped at the roots and tugged at the tangled mass and scowled . . .

'Will!' Her father was laughing. He got up to kiss her on the forehead and reach for the iron. 'You're burning a hole in my sock, Cartwheel.' He poked a finger through the hole and wiggled it at her. 'What am I going to do now? I'll have to wear it as a glove, hey, chooky?'

'Oh! Sorry, Dad!' As suddenly as it had come, Will's anxiety disappeared. All would be well. 'Sorry-sorry, hey.' She spat on the iron so that it would fizz, as a sort of full stop. 'Come, Papa. *Lezzgo*,' she said.

She took hold of his sleeve, scrunching it in her fingers and sniffing its earth-and-oil smell, and led him out into the evening air, her chin and stomach thrust forward to the dimming light.

That night, Will's father came into her room to say goodnight, which rarely happened. He un-looped the curtains, which were tied up in a knot, fingering the material. They were made of sacking – most curtains were, that Will had seen – but her mother had embroidered these with flame lilies, the national flower of Zimbabwe. Lilibet had enchanted things with her needle – when Will touched the delicate spiny red petals they felt real – and when the curtains billowed out in the wind, it was as though the flowers were blooming.

Will knew that sometimes, while she was supposed to be asleep, her father would open the door, touch the curtains and watch her, breathe her sleeping-African-child smell. She did not open her eyes beyond a crack – because if it helped him to believe she was asleep, she didn't want to spoil it – but in the light flooding from the corridor behind him, she had the impression of strong shoulders stooped, and waves of sadness, and protective love. Protection she knew she didn't need and couldn't always accept.

And he whispered, as he turned away,

'Sweetest, sweetest Lil.'

Lil was what her mother had called her; Will, Lil, Lilly, interchangeably. Hell when she was particularly exasperating. Her mother's name had also been Lil; Lilly, Lilibet, Elizabeth.

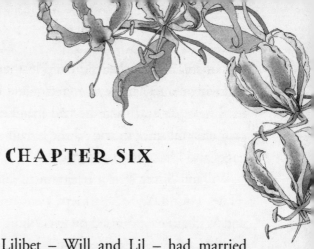

CHAPTER SIX

William and Lilibet – Will and Lil – had married young.

William Silver was born in England but bred a Zimbabwean. He loved the English hills but not the English weather: 'full of grey drizzle,' he told Will, '*grizzle*, we called it.' He sang without noticing, to his intense embarrassment, in a bass-baritone. He was, said the Harare women, 'plain as a pikestaff', 'wouldn't look twice in the street', with a large nose and large ears and a large mouth, and large hands and feet. But in spite of that, they went after him, whitened-tooth and lacquered-nail; because William was courteous, never brutal, and because he was unlikely to give, or get into, trouble. 'I'd look after him', they told each other at tea parties.

But William did not intend to be *looked after*; he wanted to do his own looking in life, he wanted to look inwards and outwards and sideways; and so when, as a young man, he *had* thus looked, and seen an advancing line of smooth plucked skin and leather handbags, he had widened his large eyes in terror and boarded a boat for England. And there he had met Elizabeth, whose skin was not smooth and whose breath smelt of green-gages and lilies, sharp and sweet.

William Silver sent a telegram to Charles Browne: 'Have Found Wife'. Farmers were used to poverty, and William economised on everything, including the word 'a'.

Browne had been sitting on the veranda, looking out at his beloved trees, when the telegram was handed to him. 'Thank you, Lazarus.' He read it, nodded, and without turning round replaced it on the tarnished silver tray Lazarus held at his shoulder. His face was suddenly stiff. 'Mr Silver is bringing home a missus, Lazarus. There is going to be a madam.'

'A madam?' Lazarus sounded dubious. And then, with new formality, he added, 'I see. A madam. Yes, boss.'

'Tell the men, will you, Lazarus?'

'Yes, boss.'

'A missus, Laz.'

'Yes, boss.'

'A woman in the house! Have to change our ways, eh, Lazarus?'

'Ah, yes, boss.'

'Lazarus –' said the Captain. He seemed to have trouble clearing his throat.

'Yes, boss?'

Browne turned creakingly round in his chair, and rubbed his pouched old eyes, and saw his house afresh. The veranda ran along the length of the main wing, giving a panoramic view of the farm; but the windows looked suddenly dirtier, the paint was more chipped, the elephant-ear plants flapped across the windows more boisterously. To him, it was perfect – but . . .

'Everything covered in dust, Lazarus.'

'Yes, boss. Sorry, boss.'

'Oh, for Christ's sake! Not blaming you, Lazarus. But – look at this . . .' and Browne allowed himself one final, rather pleasurable, shiver of sadness for what had been, just him and his men – and it was a shiver that clattered his bones together. Then he straightened in his chair, ram-rod straight, and he shook his military head, '. . . not fit for a woman.'

So the Great Scrub had begun. For two weeks before Elizabeth Silver's arrival, Browne and his men, headed by an ever-frowning Lazarus, washed and scrubbed as if the Queen of England, or the Chief of Mashonaland (the two ranked more or less equally in the Captain's estimation) were coming, rather than one awkward, hopeful young woman.

Browne fretted over fabric and worried over the washing late into the night. He struggled to under-stand the intricacies of salad forks and fish knives. He bought second-hand a book called *An Easy Guide to Etiquette*, and then burnt it in a rage: 'load of old piffling finicking fossicking bloody *rubbish*'. He walked around the bedrooms in the moonlight, touching things, reciting like a young boy at his times-tables, 'blankets, *ja*: bedhead, bedspread, bolster . . . ja . . .' He surveyed with creaking anxiety the range of female delicacies laid out on the dressing table, murmuring, 'Ingraham's Camphor Cream, Pepsodent, toothbrush, Pear's soap, talcum powder . . . is that it? Is it *right*? And is it enough now? *Is* it?'

But when Silver and his bride appeared, one look was enough to see how unnecessary it had been. She had opened the door of the car before it stopped, leapt out, fallen on hands and knees like a cat, and run on bare feet up the drive to throw her arms around the old man's neck, lifting her feet off the ground and swinging like a child. It was as if she had known him all her life.

'You are Captain Browne. I'm Mrs Silver.' Her voice, he thought, was like water running over pebbles in sunshine. And he thought, too, how absurdly young she looked to be a Mrs Anything; and although he said nothing the tips of his thought must have brushed against her, because she laughed and added, 'but you'll have to call me Lilibet. When I am fifty, *then* you may call me Missus.' She drew deep breath. 'It is *so* good to see you in the flesh. But, Captain, I have the advantage over you, because I've seen you already in everything else – in everything but flesh, I mean,' and she looked at the Captain's nicotine-stained skin, at the wrinkles and the veins, as if she ached to kiss them, 'because I've heard about nothing but you all the way from England. So of course I love you already. But you'll have to wait before you love me.'

Wordlessly, he took her hand, bowed over it, kissed it. She was wrong. He had loved her from that second.

Weeks later, Browne had watched her as she scooped him a mug of homemade soup from a tin bucket. (The bucket, he noted, was one he had bought for chilling hypothetical wine bottles. This seemed a far better use.) It was odd that the men on the farm spoke of her as beautiful, because she was not, or not really. The skin of her forehead was often spotty, and her teeth were not straight, and her features were too large for her face. Moreover, as if unable to walk slowly through a life so tremendously exciting, she ran everywhere and as a result was always bruised and scarred. Scarred, they said, but never scared. She was destined for great adventures..

Lilibet Silver, they said, knew many things. She knew how to fold the morning newspaper into a hat for the Captain; she knew how to patch up the Captain's truck with carpet and saucepan lids; she knew how to catch and cook the cane rats that ran wild in the field. She knew how to weave glass beads into bracelets that came halfway up her thin arms, which she pulled off and gave to strangers whose faces she liked. She knew how to recite poetry so that her listeners blinked and sniffed behind their tea cups, how to cut her own hair with the rusty kitchen scissors, how to out-swim the trout in the lake, how to swan-dive off overhanging branches, how to supplement coffee with chicory and make redbush tea, how to fall in love with every man she met and stay effortlessly faithful to Will's father.

Lilibet knew how to dig with an improvised spade, and which days to work in the vegetable patch. Things grew for her. Within a month of her arrival, the scrubby, dusty flowerbeds in the formal garden tumbled and bubbled into life. There were birds everywhere, lizards everywhere; Lilibet knew how to sit in absolute stillness for hours on end, so that dragon-flies and bees would perch on her neck and shoulders. It was never too late, she said, to turn a living thing around, and a garden was the most living of things. Within two months there was jasmine on every wall, and flame lilies along the veranda. Lilibet knew how to charm buds from roses that hadn't flowered for years. When Wilhelmina arrived, Lilibet knew the exact knot that would fix her baby to her back with a swathe of red cloth.

But Lilibet did not know how to remember the Nevaquin malarial tablets that newcomers to Africa must take; and she did not know how to rest and recover. Will, aged five, stumbled into her bedroom to find her father standing clutching fistfuls of the sack curtain, tears streaming down his face. His mouth was stretched open, soundlessly, and tears fell onto his tongue. Outside the window was a pool of vomit.

Neither could speak: that was the day that a silence settled on the pair of them, and they were bound close by it. Will had felt, in that moment, too small to face such misery; but she'd known that she would have to expand, now, with a terrible rush, to fit it.

CHAPTER SEVEN

Perhaps a susceptibility to malaria, rather like a susceptibility to love, is contagious. Will thought it must be.
Seven years after his wife's death, William Silver started
running a temperature. The next day, he collapsed on
the packed earth floor of the stable and was put to bed
by Lazarus, who was suddenly indignant and motherly
and stern. 'You shoulda *said* something,' he scolded
as he poured water from a tin mug on to a flannel.
'Who's going to look after the farm now, eh? You got
to stay *still* now, till the Captain comes back with doctor. Don't you *move*.' Will watched him sponge at her
father's forehead with thick fingers, more gentle now
than she had ever seen him. 'You got to get *better*, Mr
Silver.' Get better, yes: and do it better than *she* did –
Will could see the words pulsating, unspoken, in the
air.

But Captain Browne did not return with a doctor.
Instead, running down the drive to meet the doctor's
little Mazda, Will saw only the Captain's old truck, the

roar of the engine drowning the lament of the bullfrogs and grasshoppers. Through the fumes that clouded the night air, Will thought she could see a sleek female head. Will hesitated, standing on one bare foot, feeling suddenly sick. In astonishment she looked down at her hand, and saw it shaking, as from the passenger seat emerged a brisk ankle and a heeled shoe; a long, muscular calf, followed slowly by the neck and head of a woman who could only be Cynthia Vincy.

Captain Browne smiled nervously. 'Will, this is Cynthia. Cynthia, this is Will; *Wilhelmina*, of course. Not the Will that you've come for, of course . . . though I don't mean; I'm sure this Will will also be delighted; I mean . . .' He grew confused in the face of the woman's arched eyebrows, and began again. 'Cynthia has come to help us with your father, Will. She's a trained nurse.'

Cynthia smiled down at Will. The smile marred the woman's perfect poise; it was a square smile, like a letter box. Cynthia was aware of this, and rarely smiled.

'It doesn't sound too serious a case, from what Charlie has told me,' said Miss Vincy. (Charlie! thought Will in horror. She called him *Charlie*! The Captain was Charlie to one man only, her father; to her, he was sir, or Captain. Charlie!)

'These sharp attacks are the least dangerous; it's the chronic cases you need to watch. I told Charlie there'll be no need for the expense of a doctor. Don't look so sullen, my sweetie! Just money matters; nothing for children to worry about.'

'*Oh*.' Will stared up at Cynthia, at her neatly painted doll-face, and understood why she'd so hated the idea of her. She'd been right to hate her. She was shoddy.

'We'll have him up in no time, won't we?' said Cynthia, making what was evidently a *capable nurse* face. But that was a pointless sort of sentence, Will thought. There was no such thing as 'no time'. She tried to lower her voice so that only the Captain would hear: 'I think, hey, Captain . . . I don't think . . .' Will's tongue was suddenly too big, and she tried again, 'Do you think Dad – my father – will want this,' this *plastic woman*, she'd been burning to say, 'this Miss Vincy for a nurse? . . . Sir,' she added.

Cynthia gave Will a we-understand-each-other smirk. 'I know how you feel, Will. But I *am* fully capable to deal with this, I promise. And there's lots that only a woman can do in a house,' she looked sideways at Captain Browne, 'to make the men comfortable. Isn't that right, Will?'

No, it was not. Will fought the need to hit her, to set the dogs on her, to tear at her smart belted dress. No, her whole body cried, no, no! We don't want to be comfortable, go, we just want to be as we were: well, and healthy, and happy, we are so happy . . .

But the Captain looked so imploringly at her, and

he looked so frail, so oddly desperate for her approval, that Will could not move any muscle but her neck, in a quiet nod.

'Yes,' she said.

'Yes, what?' said Cynthia Vincy.

What, what? Will looked down at the mosquito bites on her arm for help, and down at her long-toed muddy feet. 'Yes, ma'am?'

'Yes, ma'am! That's *right*, Will! I like the old-fash-ioned formalities, don't you, Charlie?'

And Captain Browne, caught in the fierce beam of Will's meaning and miserable eyes, had smiled a ghastly smile and led the woman inside to the darkness of the sick man's room.

That was the first day. On the third (which to Will's bewilderment was sunlit and full of the smell of the jasmine, as if there were no father delirious behind the sacking curtains), Cynthia began to make herself felt. Simon called to Will from atop the stone wall that wrapped round the Captain's formal garden. He was writhing with laughter and with anger and barely able to keep his balance.

'She's *mad*, Will,' he said. 'The bad sort of mad. Tedias met her first. She calls him Thomas: she says she can't *pronounce* Tedias,' and Simon made a gesture to express what he thought of that. 'So I thought, OK, I'll go look at the Captain's madam. And I ran down, from the fields, fast, and I couldn't stop, and she was out picking flowers and I ran into her, boom! And she was mad like a hornet, mad like a whole nest of stingers, Will, man! And she's *huge*, Will – a proper *zisikana*, this huge woman! And she said she caught me in the private garden again – private garden, Will! Like it was hers, or something – she'd get the boss – that's what we all got to call the Captain now – to beat me. And then, ja? She smiled, and said I could tell my *little friends* that the same applies to them, and I told Peter and he said we'd put mambas in her bed, but I dunno how we'd catch them –'

He had been telling his story fast, with gestures, miming his collision, boom! – crash – but Will thought he looked suddenly darker, subdued, and he screwed up his face.

'I don't like her, Will. I . . . hope you'll be OK. And your baba, your dad, yeah? I'm gonna have to stay this side the wall for a while, ja – but remember, any trouble, and we'll get Tedias and Peter and all that lot, and we'll pull down the fence and set the bushdogs on her. Ja? OK? So – no worries, my madman.' But Simon's bravado was breaking down in patches, and he sniffed and frowned and tried to grin and then, defeated, dropped behind the wall. Will was left with a picture of a boy crouching, ill at ease, with unknown laws sweeping in on him.

On the fourth day, Will knew there was a fear in the house. The doctor's Mazda arrived at midnight, and did not leave until the next afternoon. As soon as the car drove off, Will ran to see her father, clutching a fistful of cannas and roses and grass, a bouquet from the bush, but Cynthia had locked the door from the inside. Will hammered on the heavy dark wood.

'Hello? Can I come in, ja? Hello? Papa? Dad? Please let me in, hey! Miss Vincy, ma'am, please, I've got to, please, I've *got* to come in. My dad needs to see me.'

On the other side of the door, Cynthia was winding herself into a fit of indignation. *Dad needs to see me.* It was sad, deluded. How would a scrap of a girl, not reached puberty, know what a sick man needed? She opened the door a crack. Will had not known brown eyes could look so cold.

'*Will!*' she hissed, 'Your father is asleep. But if you continue this noise, he will not be for long. If he doesn't sleep, he won't recover. And it will be your fault.' She hadn't meant to say that, but it shot out, venomously: snake-words. 'Do you want to kill him, Wilhelmina?'

On the fifth day, Cynthia herself found the door locked. Pressing her ear to the keyhole, she heard the voices of the Captain and of Silver. The Captain's voice was gruff, his breathing ragged at the edges.

'Of course I'll keep her safe, Will. You know I will. That girl . . . she's my sunlight.'

William Silver laughed, weakly. 'Would have thought you had enough of that here, Charlie,' he said.

But the Captain blinked tears from his milky eyes. 'She's sunlight and she's water and earth,' he said. 'And she's fearless. Remember when I was chewed by that hyena? Remember the blood? The shrieking? Any other child would have quailed, William; no other girl would have done what she did and washed and bandaged and sung like that. She's . . . William, if I'd had a girl, and she'd been an ounce as valiant and strong as yours, I'd be dying happy.'

Silver's face was rigid with pain, but his voice smiled. 'Ach, Charlie, I *am* dying happy.' There was a pause, while William fought for air. 'But, Charles . . . I wish I'd had longer . . . I'd have left her with . . . a mother, or a home, or . . . a future, or . . .'

'*Sus*, Will! That's nonsense, hey? Ja? Ach, William, my boy, Bill, *Will*, what are you talking about? As long as I have the farm, your girl'll have a home here. And I hope to have it to my dying day. And as for a mother . . .' His voice tailed off. Cynthia pressed herself so hard against the door that its grain was imprinted on her cheek. She thought she heard a muttered '. . . Miss Vincy . . .' But it may have been phlegm, a cough, a wheeze from an ugly old man.

The Captain lifted his voice again, unnaturally hearty. 'Anyway, Lazarus asked after you, William.

I told him he could come in later. The baccy crop's looking good, ja, and one of the mombies calved this morning. Lucian said . . .'

Cynthia Vincy had no interest in the staff. She stole away.

On the seventh day, Will was sitting by the edge of the stone pool, building pyramids of pebbles and dangling her feet in the water. Captain Browne came to find her, calling her name in a voice too weak to echo. He was thinner than ever, and his skin no longer seemed to fit. Will could see long loops of it hanging from his chin, covered with week-old stubble.

He crouched down beside her.

'*Howzit*, Will?'

'Fine, Captain. Fine, thanks.' Will was lying, and she knew she did it badly. 'And you, sir?'

'*Ja*, not bad, Will, not bad.' Then he drew breath, and looked properly at the tense, honest little body next to his. The wrists looked like skin-wrapped-glass, terrifyingly fragile. In the thin face the girl's brown eyes were bushbaby round, and her clothes had not been changed for a week. It hadn't seemed important. They fitted badly, for Will too had lost weight; for seven nights, she had shuddered in the dark, waiting, hoping, fiercely praying – a long stream of half-conscious words, 'Please, God, please, Lord, God, I need you now, God, please,' praying that her father would open the door, look in, whisper her name. He hadn't come.

The Captain laid a hand on Will's knee. 'Listen, little Cartwheel. Your father . . . it's not just a short attack. William's ill, ja? Seriously ill. Very, very seriously ill.' The Captain looked at Will, a miserable look from under bushy brows. 'Do you understand what I mean, Will?' he asked.

Yes, Will understood. And it was as though the farm and the trees and the pool had gone up in sudden flames.

'Ja,' she said. 'I understand,' and as she said it, she felt so weary and tight and small that to drop down, fainting or asleep or dead, would have been a relief. But you couldn't faint by choice.

'You OK, chooky?' The Captain had never seen anyone so white.

Will tried to nod, but her head wouldn't move. Through the ringing in her ears she could hear a terrible nothingness: no crickets sang. Will tried to speak then, in fear of this new brand of hush, tried to say 'Ja, I am. I will be. We'll be OK, sir', or just 'Yes, Captain Browne,' but the words got trapped in the back of her throat, mixed up with vomit, and Will could only mutter, choked from behind closed lips, and touch his knee; and then she ran, hard, tripping over a spade, ran out, past the limits of the formal garden, to be sick, wretchedly, behind a bush.

Lazarus, passing ten minutes later, had found her crouched on her haunches, weeping hacking sobs, roaring, spitting, crying deep rivers of tears down a dusty face. Wordlessly, but murmuring soft noises, he had gathered her up, and taken her in strong arms to his own fire, where she had wept for hours, as though her father were already dead.

So when the time had come to actually say goodbye, Will was strong again, and only her awkward, passionate love for her father was with them in the darkened room: no despair, and no strange doctors, were allowed. She kissed the frighteningly thin hands, and cheeks, and forehead and chin and lips and eyes; eyes that were open, at half-mast, and very tired.

'You look after yourself, chooky,' William Silver whispered.

Will stared at his hand, very hard. The ache in her nose and the roof of her mouth meant tears were coming. *Don't you dare cry*, she told herself fiercely. *No tears. No hullabaloo. Just love. Not tears.*

'Ja, Dad,' she said quietly. 'Will do.'

'And be good, my girl. Always goodness. Be brave. Be happy, OK? Courage, chook, ja?'

'Yes, Dad. Of course.' Her voice was wobbly, and she licked a single tear off her upper lip. It tasted of salt, and love.

'Good, and brave, and happy, little Cartwheel. *Ja?*'

'*Ja*', said Will. Her father tugged at her arm, and she bent forward. He planted one single long kiss on her forehead.

'*Ja*,' said William Silver.

After that, neither had spoken. There had been nothing they needed to say. Will knelt by the head of the bed, one hand on her father's bare chest, feeling the beating of his heart for hours and hours. Or perhaps only minutes. It was odd, she thought, but she couldn't feel time: maybe the timelessness of death was here, in the room. But eventually, her dad's eyes had closed, in sleep, or because he was dead, she wasn't sure, and she got up, and shut the door behind her, and picked up the rucksack she had packed with dried beef and flatbread and raw mealie, and, coming to the kitchen door, had climbed over it, so that it would not squeak – she could not have borne that squeak – and without stopping for a saddle she mounted Shumba and rode out into the bush.

CHAPTER EIGHT

Will returned a week later. She was hot and dry and resolved to new goodnesses, in her father's memory.

She was also newly thin, so bony she could almost smell her own marrow, and very hungry.

She stroked Kezia, who had scampered, shrieking with excitement, to greet her. '*Food*, Kezi!' she said as they ran up the path. 'Let's get us some food. What shall we have? Raisins? Bread? Cheese? . . .'

But everything had changed. Will stopped and stared. The house shone with a coat of yellow paint, and there were lace curtains at the windows, and the bushes of gooseberries that clustered round the kitchen door had been hacked into a neat, subdued line. And worst of all, when Will reached the store cupboard and pushed against the heavy metal door she found it locked. Which meant she would have to ask for the key, she knew, and that would mean going into that newly curtained main room, which, before, uncurtained, had been her own sitting room, where she had taken refuge during the rains. She had played there with her father, throwing gooseberries and grapes at each other, catching them in their mouths – and once, marvellously, she had been upside-down in a headstand, and her father had dropped a raisin down her nose. Will's nose swelled now with love at the memory; and her empty stomach felt drier, and the house stranger.

As Will approached the room – the room where, in the past, she had gone to make herself happy – she heard voices, high and sharp. She hesitated at the door, her long brown fingers hovering over the handle. It was carved silver, polished and sharp, where before it had been a brass knob that fell off if you turned it too hard. She felt her skin quiver – it was all so *new* – and instead of going in she dropped to the floor and peered under the crack.

'Oh, help. Oh, help me,' whispered Will Silver.

Twenty feet in twenty heeled shoes were elegantly crossed at the ankle, and forty chair legs were ranged in a semicircle around the empty fire grate.

She would have to go in. Will had eaten nothing all day, and her stomach was beating in time with her heart, flapping against her insides, and it was too dark now to climb the banana tree by the kennels. Will had a proper respect for darkness, and for night snakes.

The door handle was stiff. Twenty eyes turned towards her. Will was suddenly all legs and joints and was aware, as she had never been in her life before, that her hair was matted in a knot at the back of her head, and her nails were mud encrusted.

She glanced around from lowered eyes. The room had become strange. It was painfully clean. Will looked in the far corner for her cobweb collection: it was gone. The chairs had been re-covered in a dull greenish satin. It was shudderingly horrible. She would get the key, and get out.

'Miss Vincy?'

'Will.' Miss Vincy looked neither happy nor angry: just bored. 'What have you got to say for yourself?'

'I – the storeroom's locked. Ma'am.'

There was a pause. Cynthia waited, pursed lips and raised eyebrows –

'And – ?'

'And so I've not eaten all day.'

'And?'

'And so I'm very hungry.'

'And?' Was she waiting for Will to go down on her knees and beg? 'I don't – I don't understand . . .'

'I'm waiting for you to apologise, young woman, for your disappearing act. Where do you think you've been?'

Will blinked. Riding in the bush wasn't an *apologising* sort of thing: was it? It hadn't been before.

A bony woman rose from her chair and held out a plate of crust-cut-off sandwiches. 'Here, dearie.'

She had meant Will to graciously take one, but Will took hold of the plate, and would have bolted, had not an enormous woman been standing in the doorway, calling shrilly for the Staff. Lazarus had gone from *Sekuru Lazarus*, Uncle Lazarus, friend, to 'Staff' overnight.

Will retreated, still clutching the plate, into the corner of the room, sliding behind the new curtains. They smelt of chemicals and some indefinable newness, which, Will reckoned, was the smell of money. She crouched, wolfing down the sandwiches, dropping bits of cucumber down her chin, ravenous, animal-like.

The women had apparently decided to ignore her, and the high voices moved on. Will caught only words: but even that was cruel enough, hearing her father's life pecked into fragments by women like coarse-coloured hens.

'William Silver . . . you knew him?'

'. . . no money, of course . . .'

'And not much to look at . . .'

'Oh, Jackie, don't!'

'I heard different . . . and lovely manners . . .'

'Half-witted. No loss.' That was Cynthia's voice.

'Mmmm . . . But your Browne, dearie . . . a real catch, he is . . .'

'Farm valued at over a million.'

'No!' That was several voices at once.

'Yes! They lived like savages because they *liked* it, he said.'

'Cynthia'll put a stop to that.'

'And the little girl?'

'Impossible creature, I've heard.' (This in a whisper.)

'Bonny though . . .'

'*Bony*, more like.'

'And the Captain – he must be getting on, surely? Eighty?'

'Well, Cynthia's just cut out to be a widow . . .'

'People die early in the bush, sweetie!' And laughter.

There was a crash. The door burst open, hit the wall, and rebounded on to the fat woman who jumped aside. A dark woman in the doorway. Will peered from under the curtain. The woman was beautiful: she had to be some relation of Miss Vincy's; the same strong legs were there, and the wide jaw.

A hush fell. The newcomer ignored the bevy of women and spoke across the room, addressing only Miss Vincy. Her voice was soft. It commanded total silence.

'Well, Cynthia . . . it's settled. The letter came just now – your little brat's off to England. If she ever comes out of the bush, that is. It's in London. Very helpful people at the agency in Harare; nobody could possibly complain. The fees are astronomical, my dear; money puts a stop to gossip.' She laughed, a purring little laugh. 'And after that, my sweet sister . . . everything will be perfectly delightful.'

But instead of rapture or relief, the room was filling up with awkward silence. One of the women let out a single nervous laugh, cut short, like a twig snapping.

Miss Vincy gave a sigh. 'She's behind the curtain.'

The dark woman crossed the room in three paces. Will saw the feet approaching and strained away as the woman snatched back the drapes. Will froze, crouched, still clutching the plate. Such utter desolation had flooded her body that it was forcing its way out in a single, shameful tear. *Let it not be true*, she thought. It mustn't be true. What was going on? England! England was a mythic place, a huge space to make up stories about; but not to live in, not *now*; not now Dad wasn't with her, Dad who had hated it, said it was cold and full of money and cars. And *leave*! Leave the farm and the trees and the grass and Africa!

The woman's lip lifted half a centimetre in a sneer. 'Out.'

Will rose, the skin on her thigh sticking to her calves. The woman's face was hard. Was this, then, what all women were like, after the intoxicating gruffness of men? She tried to shut her nose against the sharp, synthetic perfume.

'The plate.'

Will had reached the door when the woman spoke again. Will looked at the plate, surprised it was still there; at Cynthia Vincy; at the dark woman. 'I won't!' she whispered. She was Will, afraid of nothing, Will of the bush and Will of the wind, Will who jumped down waterfalls and swam faster than Simon, Simon's best friend, and Will, daughter of Lilibet and William. She straightened her back and knees: unconsciously, she had been moving towards the door in a cramped crouch. Hot, stormy anger seized hold of her arms, and she hurled the plate to the floor, inches from the woman's feet, and it smashed into twelve pieces which flew across the room like scattering birds.

CHAPTER NINE

Within a week of Will's return, Captain Browne and Cynthia Vincy were married. It happened with the unstoppable smoothness of the inevitable. Everyone expected it.

Everyone, that is, except Will. It was too horrible to expect. But even worse, since that woman had spoken of that something – that *what*? – in England, Will had been unable to think clearly. She didn't dare ask the Captain, in case it turned out to be true. The idea of it scratched round her head, searching for a way out. Will, who was never ill, began to get headaches at night; it was, she supposed, the idea, trying to escape.

Captain Browne had not broken the news of the wedding as well as he had intended to. He was flustered and his shirt was dark with sweat patches.

'Hello, little Wildcat,' he said, and then they both flinched, because that was her father's name for her. Browne hastily amended his mistake.

'Will, my girl. You like Miss Vincy, don't you?'

The time had passed for lying. Will felt sure Cynthia Vincy had used the death of her father to worm her way into the house – why, after all, was she still here, weeks later? – she's *false*, Will thought fiercely, false as *dammit*; and she sucked in her lips and bit them together.

There was something so profoundly young about the gesture that Captain Browne was forced to close his eyes in a long blink of pain.

'Come, Will. Let's walk.'

The path led them past the rockery, past the huge aloes, past the bold colours of the strelitzias, to the bed of flame lilies. Will squatted to sniff at their growing smell, but the Captain stood rigid, staring sightlessly at the red flowers, which were curling brown at the edges. He felt unaccountably nervous.

'Will . . . chooky, I've got some . . . ah, some news, my girl . . .'

'Yes, Captain?' Will spoke very quietly. 'Ja?' She held her tongue between her teeth. It was the best way to keep the wrong words getting out.

Browne didn't seem to hear. 'The thing is, Will – Will, my girl, are you listening, hey? – Cynthia Vincy will be joining us here. Miss Vincy has said she will be my . . . wife.'

Will choked on her tongue.

'Well? What do you think of that, chook?'

'Oh.' said Will. 'Oh.' She could barely hear herself. 'Your *wife*.'

To Will the word sounded with the clang of catastrophe. And it was *ridiculous*, she cried inside; because beneath the gloss of Cynthia Vincy's nylon stockings (themselves *ridiculous* in the heat) the woman was shoddy, tawdry, empty. Will screwed up her eyes. She wondered how it was possible the Captain had not seen it. He was slow, sometimes, and cantankerous and strict, but he was generous and honest. *Wife*! She wanted to roar, to spit at him: how could he not see?

'Well, Will? What do you think?' said the Captain. He smiled nervously.

Will had opened her mouth for a bellow, for a furious, gaping *but* – but nothing came out.

'You're not making a joke, Captain Browne?'

'No, Will.' And then, after a pause in which Will stood, pulling viciously at her long eyelashes, he added, 'Nothing else to say, chooky?'

'Ja.' Will unstuck her lips. 'I hope you'll be always happy, sir,' she said.

Without thinking, only to have something to do with her hands, she pulled up a flame lily by the roots and held it out to him. He thought she looked pitifully young, standing there, dripping earth from her flower.

Awkwardly, achingly, Will tried to smile. 'Always happy, Captain Browne, 'kay?'

Exactly a week later, Cynthia Vincy became Cynthia Browne. Her first act, before she had changed out of the smart white satin suit, was to inform the Staff that the farm was to be sold. The newlyweds were moving to the efficiency of Harare, the capital city; to the street lights and air conditioning and tarmac roads of the town. Everyone expected it.

Everyone, that is, except Captain Browne. Ashen-faced, he tried to explain to his smiling wife that it would be double murder; death to the land, which needed him and his fifty years of knowledge, and death to him.

Cynthia only purred with laughter, indulgent and caressing. She'd engineered her moment with precision. Instead of the usual beer, she'd mixed the Captain a gin and tonic – a rare treat for him – and, that done, she perched on the arm of his chair, one hand on his thigh.

'And then the little girl, Charles . . .' She did not use her own name for Will, *that uncontrollable brat.*

The Captain's old face smoothed itself, and he glowed a little, as if from an inner heat. 'My Will? Ach, she's a good girl, Cynthia. I knew the day I met you, ja, that you would love her like a mother. What about my Will?'

'*Well,* Charlie. Since you ask . . .' Cynthia gave a

good impression of a woman cajoled out of her opinion. It was all in the eyebrows. 'There are some things that women know about; and I feel that your little Will – much as I would love to keep her here – can't be happy with us. Not now her father has . . .' she laid a hand on her breast, 'passed away. Just too many sad memories, don't you think?'

Captain Browne frowned. 'Oh no, my dear.'

'*No?*'

'No, pet.' Captain Browne was making the mistake of thousands of men before him: he was failing to recognise the skill of his opponent. He tried to brush her off, heartily, like a caricature of himself, 'Oh, no, my dear, Will isn't going anywhere! No, no. No! Out of the question. The girl's got nobody else.'

Cynthia laid a hand on his thigh. 'Charlie, my love. I had no idea you felt this way.'

'Well, I do, Cynthia. And you must trust that I know best, ja.'

Cynthia winced. Only common people said *ja*. 'No, Charles. It's not that simple. Because I *had* hoped,' she pouted a little, 'that what I've arranged would please you . . . I wanted us to enjoy our love, alone . . .'

The Captain looked at the blandly innocent face. A fear flickered on in his heart. 'What have you done?' he said, and added, through a sticky voicebox, 'My dearest?'

'There's a school, Charles,' said Cynthia. Her voice sank to a coo. 'A boarding school. In England. A school that's agreed to take your sweet Will at short notice. *Very* short notice. She's English by birth; she's nearing the difficult age; she'll be so much happier there. And of course you won't object, Charles, will you, not now I've settled it all?'

Browne was growing red with the weight of his unspoken protestations.

'*Cynthia,*' He could barely speak. 'Cynthia, that child . . . how could you have . . .' He looked ashen and old. 'If you knew . . . knew what she is to me . . .'

Cynthia's eyes were growing chilly. She was sick of Will: sick of the subject. Children were exhausting and tedious. 'There's nothing so hugely special about the child, Charles. School will be good for her. I've been watching her, and you should know, my *dear*, she's no genius. She's never been to a proper school, never learnt anything – nothing that takes practice. She's lazy.'

'Untamed.' And Captain Browne added to himself, *O God. I hope it will be well.*

'She has no knowledge of culture, of art, of music –'

'She sings, Cynthia. I've heard her. Sings like a bloody violin.'

'She can barely count; she knows nothing about geography, history –'

'Ja. But she's read every book in my study.'

'Exactly!' Seamlessly, Cynthia changed tack, 'So she'll need new books, won't she, Charles? And she can't use money, or hold a knife and fork properly, or,' she was running out of ammunition – 'arrange flowers . . .'

'Arrange flowers!' The Captain was suddenly austere, booming and muscular, back in his regiment, 'For God's sake, woman! Why the hell, *Cynthia*, would she want to arrange flowers? No. Will is coming with us wherever we go. You'll have to unbook the flights.'

'Charles!'

'Cynthia. I will not allow this to happen. Do you understand?'

Cynthia shook back her hair. 'Charles. Please don't talk to me like a child. I didn't want to tell you at the time; I didn't want to sound petty. Men are notoriously unjust about these things, my dear. But that plate Will broke – it was extremely valuable.'

'It was a *plate*.' The Captain tried to look unconcerned.

'No, my dear.' Cynthia put on a patient face. 'It was an heirloom. It was *symbolic*.'

'You're asking me to banish the child for breaking a plate?'

'No, Charles; it's what the plate *stands* for. If you'd seen the way she threw it at me; it was the act of a savage. She's becoming vindictive, my darling. Her father's death has warped her; she's barely human – she's running wild – and wild animals turn vicious. It has to be her or me, Charles.'

'Cynthia. Please don't threaten me. You are my wife, are you not?' The Captain blinked his old eyes, bewildered.

'I am, Charles. And I need you to treat me as a wife should be treated.'

'Cynthia! Will is the dearest thing in my life –' he saw Cynthia open her mouth – 'after you. But she is also a child, which you are not. She needs our protection.'

'*No*, Charles. She needs a new start.'

'Cynthia! This is ridiculous! I will not have it. I will unbook the tickets myself. We will not discuss it any further, please.'

'Very well.' Cynthia strode to the door and slammed it shut behind her. A painting fell off the wall. In the fields, a dog started howling. Captain Browne was just getting to his feet to follow her when she slammed in again, carrying a leather hold-all. She dropped it on his lap.

'Charles. I'm serious about this.'

'What is this, Cynthia?'

'Go on. Take a look, *darling*.'

The Captain opened the case with quivering fingers. Inside was a pile of neatly folded silk shirts, a mound of lace underwear, and three smart cotton dresses. Under the dresses were two pairs of shoes; one red crocodile skin and one black with silver stiletto heels.

'Cynthia . . . what is this? I don't understand.'

'This is my going-away bag, Charles. I do not make idle threats. It's your choice. I will leave this farm tonight, if you continue to be so ridiculously sentimental about that child.'

'Cynthia! Please. Please don't do this to me.'

'So you agree with me? About Will?'

The Captain said nothing.

'Just nod, Charles. Just nod, and I'll put away the bag forever.'

Very slowly – at the pace of ancient turtles and sunsets – Captain Browne nodded.

'Oh, *Charlie*!' Cynthia bared her teeth in a smile. She had to fight to hide her triumph. 'Oh, don't look so glum, my darling man! It needn't be forever. A year or two in civilised company, and she'll be a whole new little girl. The little Will you used to know. I've received the prospectus from the school. It's actually rather famous, amongst the right sort of person; very safe, very pretty. They had an opening for just one more pupil; little Will's an extremely lucky girl. I've already replied.' The soft silkiness of female threat came into her voice, 'I knew you would approve in the end, Charles. You do approve, don't you?'

Captain Browne set his mouth in a line.

'Oh, Charlie. You do still love me, don't you?'

Captain Browne nodded. He tried to smile. His breathing was very slow. His Will! His promise! But. His wife. His Will had attacked his wife. Life was too difficult. He stared out of the window, but his beloved trees were just a smear of green. He was getting old, and his eyes were blurred with the first tears since boyhood.

CHAPTER TEN

The next day the rains began. At breakfast the air was a solid sheet of water; by the afternoon the fields were calf-deep in mud. Cynthia would not risk her shoes in the downpour, and instead sent out Lazarus to summon Will. She was to go, he reported, *at once*, to the withdrawing room.

'The *what*?' Will dropped down from her tree, shaking the water out of her eyes. 'We don't have a withdrawing room.'

'She means your Rumpus Room, Wheel,' and Lazarus flicked his fingers by his head to indicate madness. 'That woman's bad all through. You be careful, hey?'

But Will wasn't any good at being careful, they both knew that. She was good at other things – running, and singing – and she had a sick, aching feeling that they would not help her now.

'At last, Wilhelmina!' Mrs Browne was waiting in the doorway, and she handed an envelope to Will, averting her eyes as though, Will thought, she were something particularly nasty she would rather not look at.

'This came last week. You might as well see it now. It's from Leewood College.' Will's stare widened until her face seemed all eyes. 'It's a school. In England. The Captain has decided to send you there as soon as possible.'

Will took it. She didn't want to speak to Mrs Browne, couldn't bear to show how much she cared, and she could feel that the hot storm of resentment in her chest was dangerously close to flashing out through her mouth; but she had to ask –

'Why wasn't I given it before?'

'What?'

'You said it came last week. You – shouldn't I have had it then?'

Mrs Browne sighed as if Will were being deliberately stupid.

'No, you shouldn't, Will.'

'Why not?' Will's stomach felt somewhere near her ankles. She would *not* cry.

'You forfeited the right to be treated as an adult, my dear, when you started throwing plates across the room. We knew you'd only stamp and scream when we told you. So we waited until it was all arranged.'

We? Will's head rang with the word. It meant that Captain Browne had joined in the plan to snatch Will's heart out of her chest and hurl it halfway across the world. And Cynthia Browne was not capable of understanding a creature like Will. Will had never, and would never, 'stamp and scream'. In anger she became rigid, and hushed, and lethal.

Through her daze of misery, Will got the envelope open. The letter was short and formal. It stated that Wilhelmina Elizabeth Silver, ward of Charles Browne, of Two Tree Hill Farm, had been granted a place at Leewood College, a select independent boarding school for girls. As the term had already commenced, she would be expected at the nearest possible date. Enclosed with the letter was a prospectus. It was signed *Angela Blake, Headmistress*.

Will looked at Mrs Browne: at the letter: at Mrs Browne. It was a long look; in it was everything that Will's life had been, and everything that it might have been, and everything that it would now have to be. It was a full, swollen look: a look that comprised barefoot races through torrential rain, and lemon curd eaten straight from the jar, and now aeroplanes and the coldness of English air. Cynthia Browne was unable, for some days, to sponge that look from her memory. It stuck to the walls of her head.

Will would not take the stiff, shiny prospectus into her tree house. She and Simon sat a few feet away from it, sheltered a little from the rain by a masasa tree, and pored over the paper together.

They stared at it for a long time. It was Simon who broke the silence. He swore, softly: and when Will did not reply,

'Bloody hell, Will.'

Will rolled on to her stomach and propped herself up on her elbows. The paper looked no better from the new angle. 'I know.'

'It's . . .' Simon screwed up his face. Will grasped her ankles and pulled the soles of her feet to meet the back of her head. She rocked to and fro, trying to squeeze the nervousness out of her chest.

The first page showed a dark-haired girl sitting on a sofa holding a book. There was something careful about the girl's smile. On the second page the same girl and two others were shaking hands with a tall man with grey skin. They all, Will thought, had astonishingly neat hair.

Under the photograph was a caption, '*Leewood girls meet the School Governors!*'

And she saw that the whole thing was like that: across the paper, exclamation marks abounded, like a rash. *The girls tidying their comfortable, cosy rooms! Tidy rooms, tidy minds!* And *We work hard and we play hard: Leewood girls busy with a board game!*

Other than that, there was very little writing; the

presence of the girls seemed to have crowded all the text into the bottom of the final page. Will read it quickly, scowling in concentration, gulping it in. It left an unpleasant taste in her mouth.

'Si, listen to this, ja. "The small size of Leewood College ensures that the best students are selected and the best care is given. Our girls become accomplished and successful citizens, prepared to reach fulfilment in all areas of later life". What does that *mean*? And here: "the school system aims to deal with both inter and intra-personal relations. It promotes good manners, academic excellence, and, above all, personal authenticity."'

Will stared at the paper, her forehead folding in on itself.

'Is that *English*? Si, I – I have no idea what they're talking about. I don't think . . . it doesn't sound very . . . happy. '

Simon put a finger on a picture of a girl with long plaits.

'Watch out for this one, hey. She turned too quickly, she could have your eye out with those things. '

In silence, they looked down at Will's wet hair. It was thick and very tangled, especially at the back, where Cynthia said it was *getting really shocking, Wilhelmina*. It had never been cut. They looked dubiously at the plaits. There seemed very little to say.

Simon flicked his forefinger at the photograph, at the dark-haired girl, again, with her hand high in the air. He grinned. 'Oh, *Sha.*' *Sha*, which means something like, *oh dear, oh bother,* but larger: it means, there aren't words.

'I don't think there's words for this one. Ja.' He sucked in his breath. 'Words'd be defeated before they began.'

Will nodded. Defeated, that was the word. She brushed the rain from her face. I will *not* be like that, she thought. Will caught at the thought and gripped it hard, compressed it into three words, and wrote them behind her eyes with an imaginary pencil. *I will not.*

She said, 'I'll come back, ja,' and Simon said, 'Of course,' but too quickly. She could tell when he was being polite. Neither saw a way.

'When I know how bad it is –'

'*If*, Will. It might be OK, hey. *Sha*, Will – don't decide to hate it already.'

Will shook her head. '*When* I know how bad it is – because you're not going to be there, are you?'

He punched her arm – not softly – 'No, hey, it might still be OK. There's always *might*.'

Will frowned, and then smiled a little, and kicked him. He stepped on her toe. She elbowed his ribs, but gently. He pushed her softly into a puddle. But Will couldn't find the will to fight properly: they were just going through the motions. She said again, 'When I know – I'll work out a way to get out. I'll come back. They can't stop me, ja. They can't tie me to the bed with horse-rope.'

'You hope.'

'Ja! And even if they did, I'll take a knife.'

That was an extra thing to add to the list of things to do before she left: thin out Shumba's tail, weed the giant thistles out of the flame lily bed, force the Captain to smile, find a knife, make a plan.

Simon turned the prospectus over. 'So – this is what real girls are like?'

Will tried to smile up at him. 'What does that make me, hey? Some kind of root vegetable?'

'No.' said Simon. 'You're Will.'

Will flushed. The paper of the prospectus was turning pulpy in the rain; Will tore it in two, spat on it, and hurled it into a bush. 'Come on, Si,' she said. 'Let's go.'

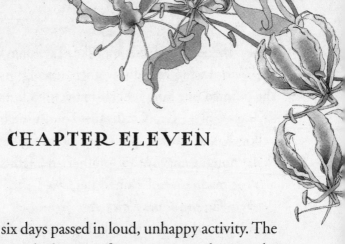

CHAPTER ELEVEN

The next six days passed in loud, unhappy activity. The farm had no telephone, so frequent trips to borrow the Madisons' were made. Airlines had to be contacted, and the farm itself put up for auction. Most urgently, Will had to be equipped with clothes for an English winter. She had never owned a coat and had only one jersey. It was six inches too short in the wrist.

It was Cynthia who took her shopping. Will loathed it even more than she had thought she would. She had not wanted to go, unwilling to spend a whole day of her last week away from the farm, 'Look, Si,' she'd planned, 'I promise I'll get through it quick. I'll come back before dark, ja, and we can roast the potatoes and we'll ride with Peter and the boys, OK? Ja?' But she had thought the actual shopping would be new and enticing.

Instead, it was humiliating. Will stood in her grey knickers in bright lights, shivering in the too-powerful air-conditioning, longing to be outside, longing for a drink, too bewildered to ask for one. Mrs Browne was brisk, efficient and businesslike. Looking neither at Will, nor at the friendly women serving in the shop, she pointed one long French-manicured finger at Will, saying: 'Skirts.' Or, 'Cardigans. Four. One blue, three yellow.' And always pointing, pointing: as though, Will thought angrily, her mother and father had had a fit of madness and named her *Shoes, Size Six, Extra Narrow Fit*; or, *White Knickers*.

Will was thrust into changing rooms and squeezed into blouses and jumpers that cost more than her entire wardrobe, and brand-new blue jeans, and nylon tops that gave her electric shocks. It was not, she told Simon later, that she hated the clothes. They were wonderful, starchy and crisp: although she would have chosen different colours: she would have liked bright orange T-shirts against light blue denim – 'to be like the sunrise, ja. Please?' – and pink trousers with grass-green jumpers, and an all-in-one denim jumpsuit like the tall, muscled mechanics wore at Tatenda Motors. But Cynthia laughed with a curled lip: 'Those are for *working* boys, my dear.' And then, Will had been astonished by the way passing women had walked in on her, had cooed over her, calling her sweet, adorable, a pretty little dear.

'Pretty little dear! You? *Sha*, Will . . . they don't know you, struze fact.'

***

The hatred did not come until later. In the dim light of sunrise, Will had found her wooden trunk – *her* trunk, the only thing she really owned, inherited from her mother – standing open outside her door, the padlock forced, and the new clothes replacing the squares of flame lily curtain she'd cut out to take with her, and the plastic bags full of masasa pods and sticks for catapults and her collection of dried mangoes. They lay in a pile on the floor.

Choking with rage, her brown eyes thin with misery, Will snatched out the now-foolish clothes – blaming the clothes themselves, swearing, how *dared* they wipe their stiff shop-smelling newness against her mother's love – and threw them into the kitchen fire. She added anything Cynthia Vincy had touched: the old dresses from the Captain, her khaki shirt, the underwear that Cynthia had washed for her – until she had only the shorts and T-shirt she was wearing. Cynthia would probably beat her. Will lifted her chin defiantly. She did not care.

Will was not beaten. Mrs Browne had been cold and rigid, icy-hard.

'You will have to learn to control yourself, child.'

'But you *broke into it*!' cried Will, hugging the padlock to her chest, 'You *broke* my lock!'

'Because – there – was – no – key.' She spoke as if

87

Will were deaf, or an unusually stupid toddler.

And Will, physically shaking, unable to see anything but mist and madness, had shouted, high and wild, '*I* had the key! *I* had the key! It was *mine*! From my mother – my mother – oh, my mama, Mum, Dad, Papa –' and Will choked, fell silent, finding that there are no words that match the feeling of *loss*, or *lost*. Loss is a vacuum, in which no living word can exist.

CHAPTER TWELVE

On the day of her departure, Will's resolution broke. Having sworn that, for the Captain's sake, she would go quietly, it felt suddenly impossible. She ran into the bush and hid; from the one adult's silky triumph, and the other's helpless regret.

Mrs Browne, stalking down from the house in a trim khaki dress, saw Will's legs hanging from the baobab tree. She set her jaw. She would be glad to see the back of those legs.

'Will!'

Will jumped. *Dammit*, she muttered under her breath. False as *dammit*. But aloud she said, 'Yes, ma'am?'

'Will, we've been looking everywhere for you! Come down! It's nearly time to go.'

'Yes, Mrs Browne, ma'am,' said Will. Time-to-go, said the beat of her heart. She dropped to the ground. Time-to-go.

'*Cynthia*, Will. I asked you to call me Cynthia.'

Cynthia Browne bared her teeth in a smile. 'Not that it matters now.' Then she looked closer at Will; something she usually tried to avoid. 'Are you planning to wear that on the plane?'

'Ja.'

'Shorts? You're going to wear filthy shorts and farm-boots on an aeroplane?'

'This is what I've got.'

'And whose fault is that?' Mrs Browne gave up the effort of her patient face. 'What was I saying? You've made me forget what I was going to say . . . oh, yes. The school has arranged for someone nice to pick you up from the airport. I've put your passport by your box. And,' Mrs Browne made gulping noise, as if to swallow disgust, 'Lazarus has put a stem of bananas out for you. They won't let you take them on board, but the man simply won't believe me that they'll feed you properly.'

'Oh,' said Will. And, 'Yes, ma'am.'

'So . . . this is goodbye then, Will.' Cynthia bent down and tried to embrace her. Will stiffened her shoulders, and she locked her hands behind her back.

Cynthia let out a little hiss of annoyance, and released her. 'I must say I'm disappointed by your attitude, Will. Look, I'm *sorry* if you're not happy with the situation . . .'

Will didn't believe it. She stared at her feet. 'Will,

these changes haven't been easy for anyone. Life,' Cynthia's voice became shrill, 'isn't easy.'

Captain Browne said the same thing, when he called Will to say goodbye.

'Life isn't all mangoes and milk tarts, Will.'

He had aged in the past months; the thin, mobile face had become gaunt. He was dressed in new trousers, new shoes – brown brogues, not his old cowhide – and he crossed and uncrossed his legs, rubbed his thighs, unable to settle.

'So it's goodbye, is it, little Cartwheel?' he said.

Perhaps the Captain saw something in the expression on Will's face at that moment, because he sighed deeply; which would not have been so bad, Will thought, except Captain Browne did not sigh. He would have said it was *dramatic and indulgent, girl*.

'Don't you worry about me, my girl. You look after you, and I'll look after me, ja?'

Or perhaps it was the way she leant toward him, one hand unconsciously held out, aching to touch him, to lay a thumb on his tired eyes and to love him back to his old, wheezing, leather-skinned, indomitable self. Whatever it was, it made him shiver, and sigh again.

'I'll write to you, my Wildcat. Cynthia thinks I should wait a month or so – give you time to settle in, ja? But after that. And you'll write to your old Captain, won't you?'

'Ja.' Will tried to smile.

'And you look after yourself. England's a good place. But don't forget how to be brave out there, Will, ja? Will?'

'Ja.'

'Right. Don't you get out of the habit of bravery. Even if you think nobody's seeing, hey? It's still so important, Will, my girl. So important . . .' His voice tailed off. He looked desperately around for something to say.

There was the sound of a car horn. The Captain touched Will lightly on the cheek. 'Safe travels, little Wildcat. Brave, remember? No tears, hey?'

Will swallowed. It was all she seemed to do these days, say goodbye. She'd worked out that silent partings were easier than noisy: there was less to regret. She nodded. 'No tears, Captain Browne.' She stood on tiptoe to kiss the rough-stubbled cheek. Then without another word, without looking up again at the old face, Will walked out to the waiting car.

There she stumbled, brought up short. There had been two car journeys into town (for the shopping, and for a passport photograph. Will liked the photo. Her bird's nest of hair stood up at the back like a halo, and she was scowling ferociously, because the jolly photographer kept telling her to 'say chongololo') and for both they had taken the Captain's rusty red Toyota pickup. It had smelt of petrol and sawdust, and Cynthia Browne had sat in the front with gritted teeth, but for Will it had been the best part of each expedition, a tooth-rattling ride in the open back with a gang of farmhands. Will had looked forward to the drive to the airport; 'It'll be my Last Ride,' she said to Simon – they spoke about it in capital letters. 'Ja – it's going to be wind-rushing and bumpingly-good; it'll be my Ride Out of Africa.'

But the car that waited in the drive was a hire-taxi, large and monstrously sleek. It was the sort of car that mustn't be scuffed and mustn't be smudged. Nobody had ever sung in that car, or wound down the windows and perched on the sill and snatched at fruit from the trees by the side of the road. Will felt, with a new coldness in her chest, that when she climbed in she would be opening the door to a new way of being. It would be a different version of reality. And any world that you reached this way, through chrome and a smell of leather (it was a smell of *false*, she thought; a smell that bypassed nostrils and shot straight to the brain) could not be a good world. It was that simple.

The boys had gathered to see her off. Will had already given out her parting presents. She didn't have much she could give; her most treasured possession was her box full of books, which none of the boys wanted. In the end she forced Simon to take them, with strict instructions to teach the younger ones to read. To Lucian Mazarotti, she gave Shumba's saddle and reins, and she would have given him Shumba, but she wasn't sure he was hers to give now. To Tedias she gave her precious green tin mug and her collection of cricket balls, and she had sewn her sheet into a shirt for Lazarus. To Simon, best of all, she gave Kezia, and now the monkey hung from Simon's neck, chattering nervously, perhaps picking up the stiffness that had come over the children.

Simon had given Will a torch. 'The batteries aren't great, hey,' he had said. 'It's a bit flickery. But they probably have loads of batteries in England, ja.' She had felt oddly swollen in her chest. It had been one of his most treasured things, because it meant light at night without smoke.

As she approached the car, Simon held out a small parcel wrapped in newspaper and strong sisal grass. 'I made it for you, Will. I . . . ah . . . ja. You don't have to open it now.'

But Will was already tearing at the paper. Inside was a little cat carved out of limestone. It had an arching back and pointed ears. 'Tedias helped. It's a wildcat. Because of what your father called you, ja? To remember us.'

'OK. Ja,' said Will. She held it to her chest. And then, 'Thank you, Si. I like it. I – ja. Thank you, hey.'

His face was scrunched up, his nose flaring in and out to control emotion.

'Miss you, Will.'

'Miss you, Si.'

And as Will climbed into the evil-smelling backseat, he leant in through the open window, and whispered, spraying her with excitement, suddenly fierce, 'I'll give her a headache and a half, Will; *struze* fact. We'll send her proper mad.'

He thumped the bonnet of the car. The engine started.

'You be happy, madman!'

And Will, leaning out of the window to wave, shouted back,

'*Faranuka*! Simon, boy, *Faranuka*! Lazarus, *Faranuka*! Lucian Mazarotti! Peter, Thomas, *Faranuka*!'

The car gathered speed, and the host of barefoot boys ran down the dust-track after the car, tapping the boot, and then falling back, ululating and laughing.

And then the car left behind the farm and Will's sunlit childhood, and the only way of being that she had ever known.

'*Faranuka*.' It meant *be happy*. And what other choice was there, in a world like hers?

CHAPTER THIRTEEN

Will's first sight of the school was coloured black with rain and cold and misery.

She ran straight past the man sent to pick her up at the airport, tripping over her shoe laces and stumbling past rows of exhausted-looking people. She wouldn't talk to anyone: she'd just find a corner and wait until someone came for her. Will closed her eyes and brought her knees up to her chin and bit on them, hard. It left bite marks on her skin, but it was a way of ignoring the terror in her chest.

This, it turned out, was the wrong thing to do. When the stewardess and the driver found her half an hour later, crouching under one of the long airport benches, they said so. Will stared wordlessly at them as they said it several times over, in unison, like a fretful duet. The man sent by the school brandished a sign at her. It said, '*Wilhelmina Silver. Leewood School.*'

'Didn't you see the sign? Do you speak English?'

Will struggled to speak. She could only bite the inside of her cheeks.

'Oh, Lord Almighty,' he said. 'What do they speak in Africa? Parlez-vous Anglais?'

Will nodded, but found she couldn't find words. She wanted to explain that her name was *Will* (or Wildcat; or Cartwheel; but she kept herself from saying that); he had turned away, looking for her luggage. She tried to apologise; but his large square back was already receding, and she had to run to keep up.

The man remained brittle and tight-lipped for the drive, which was endless and swerving and so fast that Will's stomach was feeling green and swollen before they were halfway there.

At home the roads were mostly potholed and dusty, and the tractors and trucks travelled over them slowly. Will had always thought they looked like fat fastidious women, and when she was allowed to drive the pickup along the more deserted tracks she made dirt spurt and the air whip by with speed – but even then she couldn't coax the speedometer past forty. Now she pulled her legs up to her chest and hid her head between her knees and tried not to think about her father sitting in the passenger seat, laughing, with one hand hovering over the emergency brake.

The driver was watching her in the mirror. But, 'Feet off the seats, please,' was all he said.

Will had not thought her heart could ache more. It felt red-raw, like a popped blister. Then as the car pulled up at the school gates, she saw she was wrong. Her heart clenched like a fist. Will hunched further into her corner and stared. She stared so long that her eyes turned dry and prickling. It was pure ugliness, she thought desperately; it was misery in concrete form. Everything was grey – the square main building, the benches, the bark on trees, and spread out above the school, the grey sky – everything was the colour of an old photograph. Will tried to breathe properly.

The man pulled up outside the largest of the buildings.

'Out you get. That's right. Mind the leather.' Will stumbled, tripped over the metal doorframe, and flinched away from his supporting hand.

He looked pointedly at the mud her boots had left behind. At home, Will thought, mud was to be cultivated and adored; mud and water and the sun and mango trees: they went together.

There were no children in sight. The man looked at his watch. 'Twelve o'clock. They'll be in class. They expected you by morning break.'

Will didn't speak.

'Never mind; can't be helped.' He looked curiously at her. What sort of child stood so still? 'Wait here while I park the car. Sit on that bench; by the playground; there. That's right. Don't move. I'll be right back.'

As she climbed out of the car, it started to drizzle. Grey drizzle: Will felt herself smile a tiny smile at the thought: grizzle. Her legs were stiff and heavy after two days and a night of sitting still. Experimentally, she waggled her ankles. They still worked. Slowly, she walked up and down the tarmac, breathing in rain and air. It wasn't like African air; it was thicker, and smelt of rubber and something sharp; but still . . . Will took in gulps of it. It was air. Air was beautiful.

Her legs still seemed to be warming up, so she sped up; she tried to practise her handspring, but the concrete was cold and shards of it stuck to her hands. She ran instead, and forward-rolled and star-jumped until she felt warmer and she could jump and touch her toes in the air. She cartwheeled; and her hair flew out behind her just as it had at home. (Gravity still functioned then, she thought. That was something.) There was a leafless tree growing against the largest of the school buildings: she pulled herself up into it, and breathed the living-bark smell. She jumped down, put both ankles behind her head and rolled around the tarmac. Then she stood on her head against a bench until her face turned red. Her limbs stopped feeling like chair legs. Her heart started beating again.

Faces appeared at a window overhead. Will didn't see

them; she kept cartwheeling, faster and faster round the edges of the asphalt playground.

'Who's *that*?'

'Look at that! How does she do that?'

'Did you see that, Sam? Is that the new girl?'

'Look! Samantha! Did you see that, Sam?'

The girl called Samantha gave a chilly little laugh. 'So what? I can do that.'

'*Really*?'

'Yes, really.' Samantha blew on the glass.

'Sam! Now we can't see!' Another girl started scrubbing at the mist.

'I hate people who show off.' Samantha was the tallest by a head. Everyone agreed she was the beauty of the year.

Almost everyone. One girl said, 'But she doesn't know we're watching.'

'So?'

'So, she can't be showing off, can she?' and the girl's twin added, 'You can't be showing off if you're by yourself, can you?'

'Shut up, Hannah.'

'But you can't!'

'Shut up, Zoe.'

Below them the driver reappeared, and said something to the girl. They watched through the glass his mouth open and shut like a goldfish; saw him tap his watch and his shoulders heave a sigh; and they saw the girl guiltily scramble upright and follow him, brushing tarmac stains from her palms and smiling a tiny secret smile to herself.

CHAPTER FOURTEEN

Will was handed from the driver to a tall, distracted-looking head girl who led her down dark corridors; from the head girl to a prefect, and more corridors; and from the prefect to two girls her own age. It was like the luggage carousel at the airport, Will thought. Only nobody seemed to want to collect her.

'This is Samantha, and this is Louisa.' The prefect sniffed at the air above Will's head. 'And this is Wilhelmina. Samantha's the student representative for her form. Louisa's –'

'I'm Sam's best friend,' Louisa broke in. 'And classroom monitor for the term.'

'*One* of my best friends.' The girl called Samantha didn't look so keen, Will thought. She had a nose that turned up at the end, and very white teeth. Both had tidy faces and hair pulled back – like a horse's tail, Will thought, but so *neat*. 'You're Wilhelmina Silver?'

That emphasis on *you're*, Will thought, was not friendly.

'It's Will,' said Will. She tried to smile, but something was wrong with her muscles. 'I'm Will.' She tried again, to say, 'Hi. *Ja*. I'm Will. *Manheru*.' But her face kept crumpling into wary misery.

The girls looked at each other, unsure. 'Sorry, you're *what*?'

'I'm –' Will stopped. What was she? 'I'm never called Wilhelmina; it's Will, ja; or my Dad calls me Will o'the'wisp, or Wildcat –' She'd got the tense wrong. *Used* to call me. Will bit her teeth together so her jaw jutted. She whispered to herself, *hush. Hush, hey. Stop talking. Stop panicking.* Her brain seemed to have been cancelled out by desperation and sadness.

The two girls exchanged looks. 'Right,' said the first girl. 'Will? Like the boy's name?'

'Yes. Will. Like the verb, ja?'

'Right.' Samantha's eyebrows disappeared into her fringe.

The other girl, Louisa, said, 'Um . . . Is that what you're wearing?'

'Yes.' Obviously it was. Will stared at her shoes.

'We have to wear uniform, you know,' they said together. 'It's the *rules*.'

'Ja. OK.' She wondered why they put such emphasis on the word 'rules'. She felt her knees shiver.

'Have you ordered a uniform?'

'Ja. I think so. Yes. Someone has.' Will hoped it was true.

'And aren't you freezing? You're wearing *shorts*.' Will couldn't have said why, but in Samantha's voice the question sounded like a taunt.

'Ja. I know.' Will tried to smile. They didn't smile back. She wasn't surprised: it was a false smile, she thought, false as *dammit*, so she scowled at the floor instead.

'Well,' said the one called Samantha. 'You'd better come with us, I guess.'

Will followed them through two more corridors. She sniffed them, trying to get a feel for the place – they smelt horribly of *clean*. The girls stopped at an office with a glass door. Through it she could see thick carpet, books, papers, and a computer. Everything was ranged neatly on shelves, at right angles to everything else.

'This is Miss Blake's office. Miss Blake's the head-mistress.'

'Ja. I know. She sent us a letter. She has beautiful handwriting.'

'She does that for everyone.'

'Oh,' said Will.

'She's not in.'

'Oh,' said Will again. They seemed to be waiting for more, so she said, 'Ja. I can see.'

'She won't be back until tonight. But Mrs Robinson – that's her assistant – will be here in a second. She must have given up waiting. Because you're late, you know.'

Will tore at the skin around her nails instead of replying. The girl pursed up her mouth, like a disapproving adult – or, no, it's like a goat's little pink sphincter, Will thought. She held back the urge to spit.

'Very late, actually,' said Samantha.

'Ja,' said Will. The skin round her nails started to bleed. 'I know. We had to stop the car.'

'Why?'

She could feel herself flush. 'I was sick on the seat.' The girls smirked. 'It wasn't on purpose, ja. Not everything I do's on purpose.' The Captain used to say she was like a hurricane. Will the Wind, he said; and the wind smashed things and blew them over; but it also made kites fly. He'd said that when she'd used the larder shelves as a ladder and smashed forty-seven jars of jam, and he'd walloped the back of her head and rubbed her hair and let her go. Remembering, Will's chest tightened. The loneliness made it hard to breathe.

'Oh,' said Samantha. 'Couldn't you find a sickbag, or something?'

'No.'

'You've got sick on your jumper, did you know?'

'Oh,' said Will. 'Ja.' She hadn't known. Furtively, she scrubbed at her front.

Samantha smiled. Her eyes were sharp. She was,

Will thought, like *tin*. Or glass. If you tapped her with a fork, she'd *ping*. 'It's not exactly elegant, is it?'

It had never occurred to Will. She said, 'No. Ja. I don't think I'm designed to be elegant.'

The girls exchanged glances. 'We'll find Mrs Robinson.'

Louisa said, 'You stay here. *Stay*.' As though Will were a dog.

As they turned to go Samantha added, 'By the way, Will. Did you know you've got mud all over your shoes? And all up your shorts?'

Will stared. Of course she knew. 'Ja. That's what boots are for.'

She hadn't noticed, until now, that the two girls did not wear boots, but black patent leather shoes that shone. And she could see, now she was looking, how pretty they were. They wore short green skirts and white shirts – not shirts like her father's: these were stiff, all angles and corners – and everything about them gleamed: their skin, their hair, their little glinting earrings. Their nails were the pink of bubblegum wrappers. The Captain's nails were green from fungus rot; Will thought possibly these girls had a similar sort of disease. As they turned away she heard a snort, and a laugh.

'Did you *smell* her?'

Will sank down against the wall and closed her eyes.

She pressed handfuls of her hair to her face, and tried to breathe without the catch in her throat. She counted to a hundred; in English, and then in Shona. She had just reached makumi mapfumbamwe nepfumbamwe – ninety nine – when she heard footsteps approaching, and opened her eyes. She was looking at an advancing woman with large hair and a small, thin smile.

'There you are, my dear!' The smile stretched even further. 'You must be Wilhelmina Silver.'

The woman wore a stiff white shirt that buttoned up to the neck. Her head sat on top of it like an egg on an egg cup. As Will scrambled up from the floor, she wondered feverishly if she should hold out her hand. Did they shake hands here? Kiss? Rub noses?

'You are Wilhelmina Silver?' said the woman. She looked closer at Will and stopped smiling.

'*Yes*,' said Will. It came out louder than she'd meant and Mrs Robinson stepped back, as though expecting her to bite, or scratch. 'Ja. I am.'

'Oh.' Mrs Robinson did not smile. Will discovered later that Mrs Robinson avoided facial expressions: she believed they caused wrinkles. Instead, the woman stared at the knots in the young girl's hair, and the scratch on her cheek. Will wondered why Mrs Robinson didn't meet her eyes.

'I see. Well. Go in, go in.' She flapped her hands, like Lazarus herding the bantams. 'Have a seat, my dear. No, sit up properly, please. Properly. That's it. Feet off the seats, if you don't mind.'

I *do* mind, Will thought – she minded this woman, horribly – but she sat up ram-rod straight, holding her breath.

'Now, I wanted to see you privately, my dear, before I let you run off to lunch and get to know the other girls. Your guardian . . .' Mrs Robinson consulted a piece of paper, 'Mrs Browne – mentioned in her letter that there might be problems with your attitude to the school.' Mrs Robinson smiled without troubling to involve her eyes or forehead. 'We know you've had a very tough time recently, haven't you, pet?' She waited for Will to reply. Will kept holding her breath. 'Haven't you?'

From where Mrs Robinson sat, Will looked sulky. She was also too short and thin for her age, and the state of her hair was an abomination. Her voice was a few degrees colder as she said, 'And you'll work with us to smooth out those problems, won't you, Wilhelmina?' Will let out her breath in a rush and felt her toes curl inside her boots. 'I know you'll try to fit in here. Won't you, Wilhelmina?'

Will bit her lip hard. She thought, *courage, chook*. She could taste blood; and cold air; and bewilderment.

'Please answer me, Wilhelmina. You'll try your very best to fit in, won't you, my dear?'

Will couldn't say she would fit in. *Fitting* was what lids did to jam jars. Instead she said, 'Could I go and find my suitcase? Please, ja? It's got my jersey in it.' She held out her hands, which were blue at the tips. 'I'm very cold.'

Mrs Robinson sucked in her breath. Will said more quietly, 'Can I go? Ja? Please?'

'I suppose so. Off you pop then. And welcome, my dear, to Leewood.'

CHAPTER FIFTEEN

Another prefect – identical to the first: tall, pretty and apparently painfully bored by Will – led her through more corridors, up two winding staircases, more corridors. (The buildings were a maze of corridors: if you'd stretched them out, she reckoned you could've got halfway across Harare.) A third prefect – this one plumper and darker than the other two – appeared from the library and led Will on, up to the Residency. It was a square building, like a tobacco barn at home, Will thought, but with a slate roof instead of tin.

The girl said, 'This is where we sleep. The toilets are all in the main block. It gives you good bladder control.' She smiled. Will tried to smile back; but she knew it must have been a failed attempt because the girl sighed. 'Come on. They left your suitcase at the bottom of the main stairs.' She tried to take Will's hand, but she shook her head and held it in a fist behind her back. When they reached Will's suitcase, she tugged her one warm cardigan from it and clutching it to her chest followed (more corridors; more smell of cleaning fluid; more staring girls) to the dining hall.

'You just take whatever you want on a tray – there, from that pile; and cutlery's over there – and go and sit with your form. That's them; in the corner; see?' The girl seemed eager to get away. 'You'll be all right from here? Why are you staring? You don't need looking after, do you?'

Will shook her head. She'd never been *looked after* in her life. She edged past the gangs of bigger girls; past a forest of green skirts; and stopped, stock still, gaping with the strangeness of it. She'd never seen so much food in one place. There was a sweating woman ladling stew and rice on to plates. There was fruit, peeled and sliced into pieces, swimming in syrup; she'd never seen anything like that. At home, fruit just came off branches into your hand. Peter, who was fussy, used Will's penknife to chop out the bad bits; the others ate round them or spat them out. Will ran from one side of the counter to the other; here there were plastic pots with 'fromage frais' printed on the side – Will decided not to risk those – and glass bowls of chocolate whipped into brown fluff, with sprinkles and whipped cream. At home chocolate came in thick bars, and she hesitated. It was so pretty that she wasn't sure if it could be edible. She dipped a finger into one and whispered, '*Sha.*' It was like a chocolate cloud. She took two more bowls, and then, as she went by on a second circuit, a third. She was starving.

The sea of faces turned towards Will as she approached the table. She couldn't meet anyone's eye, but she could feel the whisperings rising like a tide as she sat down. Will could not block her ears and eat at the same time; so she put her right hand over her head and ate with her left.

There was a wave of laughter, and gasps.

'*Excuse me*, my dear!'

Will looked up from her stew. The teacher sitting at the end on the table had nostrils that were white and thin and clenched; Will braced herself to run. She knew she must have done something terrible.

'We eat with our forks here, please, dear, or we don't eat at all. We're not savages, are we, now?' said the woman. She looked closer at Will. 'Are you new, dear? What's your name? We haven't seen you before, have we?'

Will's ball of rice had dropped from her fingers. She tried to cover it with her arm as she said, 'Will. I'm Will, ja. I –'

'Oh, dear! Get a cloth and wipe that up, Will. And I'd like you to wash your hands and face, please, before you come back.'

Will turned away from the snortings and spittings of laughter as she pushed back her chair.

'My God! Did you *smell* her?' Will did smell, she knew: of woodsmoke and Kezia and grass. Her boot connected with the girl's chair leg as she passed; but then her chest burnt and flushed with shame and she latched her fingers into a knot so they couldn't strike out. Will only fought her equals.

'Like a savage. Do you think she bites?'

'Is *that* the new girl? I thought it was the cleaner's daughter.'

'Looks like she belongs in a *zoo*.'

'I thought Samantha was exaggerating!'

'I *told* you so!' That was Samantha.

'Did you see her shoes?'

'Is she wearing *shorts*? In winter?'

'Did you see what she was eating? Four chocolate puddings. She'll get fatter than Sofia.'

'And did you see her *hair*? She could have a nest of rats in there.'

'Bet she doesn't wash.'

'Bet she's got *nits*.' Will tried to run, but her laces were tangled and she tripped.

'What's wrong with her?'

'Do you think she's mad?'

'Do you think she's dangerous?'

'Hold your breath, she's coming.' One made gagging noises.

Will couldn't bear it. She put her hands over her ears

113

and hurtled down along the last tables of girls and out into the playground.

It was drizzling and deserted, and the tarmac was cruel and icy when she sat on it. She struggled to force back the embarrassment, but it insisted on rising up from her chest and out through her eyes. The Captain insisted on forks, but her father did not. Tears worked their way into her mouth and she sniffed. The woman had been wrong. Simon and Lazarus never used forks, and neither did Shumba or Kezia or Will.

The rain fell more heavily. Will crouched, African-style, with her back against the wall and her chin on her knees, breathing quick, shallow breaths. Her chest felt hollow, and she had never been this kind of frightened before: shocked and shy and bewildered. This was not the marvellous-mad-adrenalin fear of snakes, or the rollicking fear of an unruly horse. It was something else.

Will wasn't sure how long she squatted there, alone in the wet. She could feel she was on the brink of falling into miserable sleep in the rain when an alarm sounded, high and shrill across the playground. Like a cat Will was up, and tensing and tightening her grip on her bag and ready to run if it meant fire or raiders or flood. The bell kept ringing. Oddly, there were no screams.

A girl appeared; one of the twins she had seen at the

other end of the table. She stared at Will's dripping taut face. 'Hello. You're Will, aren't you?'

'Ja.' Will pulled herself to her feet.

'Hi. My name's Hannah. They said I had to fetch you for maths. The bell's just gone.'

'Oh.' Will unclenched her fists. '*Oh.*' There were purple ridges along her palms where her nails had bitten her skin.

Hannah appeared to be embarrassed about something. 'Will? I don't want to be rude – but – did you know you've got stew in your hair?'

'Oh. Ja. I did.' Will lied. She put her hands to her face but she was drenched and shivering and her fingers were numb and she could have had a three-course meal on her head and not have felt it. Will smiled, a little, at the thought, and the girl must have thought it was aimed at her, because she smiled back, showing metal on her teeth.

'Are you going to wash it out?'

'Ja, of course. I *do* wash. Sometimes. But there's not time now, is there?'

'No, I suppose not. Wait a second, though. Hold still.' Will saw she was taking out a brush from her backpack and without thinking she backed away and let out a little cry. She couldn't bear strange hands, now.

Hannah looked astonished. 'I wasn't going to hurt you!'

Will had no idea what to do. She said, 'Oh. I –. Wait – I didn't mean . . .'

Hannah didn't turn round. 'Come on. It's fine. If you want to be called a savage, that's not my business.'

In the classroom Will was given a desk with a fake-wood top, a plastic pen and a book. The teacher sat at the head of the room; if, Will thought, she could spend the day reading, not talking to anyone, it wouldn't be so heart-numbingly bad. With rising hope, she opened the book.

It was a mess of numbers.

Will said several forbidden words under her breath. '*Oh penga.*'

The girl next to her was staring. 'Did you say something?'

'Nothing. I – no, nothing, ja.'

'Really?' The girl turned round in her desk to make expressive faces at the girls behind. 'Right. We're not really supposed to talk, you know.'

Will could add and subtract and she knew, in theory, about multiplying. But there were letters, here, mixed up with the numbers; it made no sense. She forced herself not to panic. She rubbed the paper between her fingers. It didn't become clearer. She scratched it with her thumbnail. She smelt it. It was still incomprehensible.

According to the name at the top of her worksheet,

the girl next to her was called Joanna. She had red hair and very small eyes. She looked over Will's arm at her blank page and laughed.

Will said, 'What?' She allowed herself to half-smile. 'Ja? What's so funny?'

'Nothing.'

'What, ja?'

'You! You can't do basic algebra.'

'*Oh.*' Will sat on her hands. 'Is this algebra?'

'Very *basic* algebra. We don't do proper algebra until Year Nine. Can't you even do long division?'

Will said nothing; she fought hard not to jab her pen into Joanna's face. Joanna said, 'Do you know quadratic equations? I do.'

'What're they?'

Joanna smirked. Will did not roll up her exercise book and force it up Joanna's nose. She whispered instead, soft, behind her hair: 'truth, hey, dear heart, and courage'. It did not work.

'Oh, God!' said Joanna. 'You needn't cry. Just because you don't even know your times tables.'

'I'm not crying,' Will said, 'and ja, I *do*, actually.' It was a lie. Could other people tell if you were lying? 'I *do* know my times tables.'

But in fact, as the day went on, it became obvious to Will that she knew nothing. At every lesson they made her sit at the front, in the middle of the row – 'just until you settle in, Wilhelmina,' and the girl they had forced to sit next to her would edge away and make expressive faces at her friends and then sigh and say, 'Miss Smith!' or 'Mrs Robinson!,' or 'Miss Macintosh! Will can't do the work.'

In that grey blur of a first day, Will learnt many things. She discovered that times tables had nothing to do with time, nor, in fact, with tables; that history was not (as Lazarus had said, and she'd believed him) a thousand stories building up into the colossal, strange, heart-stoppingly-beautiful tower of the present; that knowing about cows and snake bites and birth and umbilical cords was irrelevant in science class. She learnt also that her shorts were wrong and she had gypsy-hair and she wasn't funny, wasn't clever, and looked like a mad tramp in her thick socks and muddy boots.

They came upon Will after dinner, crouching on a toilet lid and eating a hot chicken breast with her fingers. Samantha called the others, Joanna and Louisa and Bex, to watch. They were pretty even when they jeered.

'I hate them,' whispered Will. The hair on her arms stood up when they came near.

CHAPTER SIXTEEN

It was terrible, too, at night.

Miss Blake, the headmistress, escorted Will to her bedroom personally that first day – an honour, though Will didn't know it. Mrs Robinson walked on her other side; like a prison guard, Will told herself.

'This will be your room, Will; and that's your bed.' Miss Blake had dark hair and lips the colour of a flame lily. She was the only colourful thing in the room, Will thought. 'You should be pretty comfortable, I hope, once you get used to the detergent smell. I don't suppose you had Persil in Africa. Beds are like shoes, Will, they need wearing in.'

Will wasn't listening; she was looking. The room was tiny and dark. There were burglar bars on the window. Somewhere above her head, Mrs Robinson was saying something about lights out at nine, and not wasting water. The room smelt foul, Will thought: of eggs and feet and the eternal indoors. It was the smell of *English*. She edged to the window and looked out: there was a car park, a crisp packet and a very flat pigeon. Two of the three beds were surrounded by photographs of men and women and blonde girls torn from magazines. Will touched one; they all had careful smiles and odd, fake-looking skin.

'Wilhelmina! Please don't touch other people's belongings.' Mrs Robinson's voice was sharp. 'We need to have rules, Wilhelmina, and respect for others is one of the most important. Come here, and unpack. I see you're nice and snug in the corner.'

The third bed had her suitcase on it, and a bedspread that was probably meant to be a calming shade of nothing. It was the colour of a rat's tail.

Miss Blake smiled from the doorway. 'You'll share this with Samantha and Louisa; Mrs Robinson thought, as you met them first, that would be easiest. Take your time unpacking. There's no hurry.'

'Ja.'

'And you must tell us if there's anything you need. We're delighted to have you, Will.'

Will tried to reply, but by the time she had untangled her brain enough to talk, Miss Blake was gone. Desperate, Will caught Mrs Robinson by the sleeve as she went out. 'Please, ma'am . . .'

'Yes, Wilhelmina? You know, you don't need to say ma'am. Call me Mrs Robinson.'

'It's just . . . they promised, at the farm, ja? That I'd

be able to sleep where I liked. Outside, Cynthia Vincy said. She *promised*. I'll . . . I can't . . .' To her fury Will found she hadn't words. The room was so small; and with those windows; it was a cage. It would be like sleeping in a nightmare. 'Can I have a bed by myself? Outside? I could make a tent? Please? Or even I could sleep in a tree, with my blankets? Please? I won't sleep in that room.'

'Wilhelmina! Please, my dear, have a little sense!' Will watched, desperate, as Mrs Robinson's glasses misted with amusement.

'*Please.*'

'Can you hear that, Wilhelmina? It's hailing.'

'I wouldn't care, ja. I could buy an umbrella.'

Mrs Robinson laughed. Her laugh, Will thought, was extraordinary. It involved none of her facial muscles. 'I'm afraid that's just not practical, my sweet.' She paused in the doorway. 'This is England, my dear! This is the land of common sense.'

Will had nightmares that first night. Samantha and Louisa took from under their pillows cotton suits patterned with rosebuds. Will watched from her corner, fascinated.

Until Samantha said, 'What are you staring at? Don't you have pyjamas?'

'Pyjamas?' Will stopped with her T-shirt half over her head.

'What do you sleep in in Africa?'

'In – in my knickers.' Will could feel her face flaming.

'That's disgusting.' That was Samantha.

'Yeah. That's *disgusting*, Will.' That was Louisa, Samantha's echo.

'You can't sleep in your knickers here. It's against the rules.'

'Is it? Are you sure?' Will couldn't remember it being on the list stuck to the door.

'I *said* it is, didn't I? You can't sleep like that, all right? You don't want me to have to put glue on your flannel.'

Will said nothing. Every finger and every muscle was trembling with exhaustion. She put back on her damp socks, her wet jersey. She laced up her boots and lay stock still in bed.

'Is she wearing her *boots*?'

'D'you think she's contagious? Can you *catch* madness?'

Will put her hands over her ears. She could still hear them.

'Savage.'

'*Tramp*. Filthy little tramp.'

'Freak.'

'Midget. Midget-freak. Dirty *savage*.'

She fell asleep with their voices jabbing at her heart, and dreamt of being chased through the bush by a pack of wolves, with sleek ponytails and rosebud pyjamas.

CHAPTER SEVENTEEN

Every night Will felt she couldn't face another day. Every day she felt she couldn't face another night. Inexplicably, her body refused to die of a broken heart.

It was unrelentingly bad. Daily, Will added to her collection of rebukes. In lessons the teachers sighed and smiled and looked pitying. The girls stared, giggled: stared again. Will realised she'd never been so watched before. Her days had been her most precious secret. But it was impossible, here, to be alone. And everything she did was wrong.

'Sit up straight, please, Wilhelmina!'

'Will! Second warning! Feet off your chair!'

'Don't chew your ruler, please, Will. That's better. Show some respect for school property.'

'This is a group exercise, Will.' Miss Blake, who took them for English once a week, smiled her kindest smile. 'No thoughts at all to share with us?' Will's chest was full of hot humiliation and claws and crow's beaks on those days; and her face set into an awkward frown.

And then there was, 'Don't doodle, Will. Just do the work, please,' though she had no idea where to start. She would, she thought, rather catch a water scorpion with her bare hands than struggle, blushing with shame, through double maths. After a week, they began to lose patience. '*Do* try not to daydream, Will. Your desk is not your bed.' And once, sharply, 'Keep your eyes on your own work, Wilhelmina! This is a test,' and Will flushed with shame: at being caught; at the hissing laughter from the back row; at the unhappy shock of the twin next to her, who shielded her paper with her arm and looked away; worst of all, at what her father would have said. She sat on her hands and whispered, *Penga. Penga, booraguma.* Wildcats do not cheat.

Worst were the classes with Mrs Robinson. 'Sit *down*, Will. You can't just walk out of the classroom when you feel like it.' Mrs Robinson had the shortest temper of them all. 'The toilet? Is it desperate? Go on, then.' Will got lost, and had to climb out the window of an empty classroom and crouch behind a bush; and Samantha, who had followed, gleefully told the others. They slipped notes into her books, written in jabbing capitals that cut into Will's chest: *stinking SAVAGE. Filthy tramp.*

It was no easier outside of the classrooms: worse, she thought.

Will didn't have a bright plastic pencil case, or money to buy one: she looped her pen and pencil and pencil sharpener together with an elastic band. Samantha ran her fingers over her glitter pens and smiled pityingly.

At break times, Will crouched in the triangular spaces behind doors with her books. They always found her. Samantha led them; tall, almost unbearably pretty, with pink lips and cheeks and the beginnings of breasts. Prettiness seemed the only criteria for success here. They had little tubes of ink for their fountain pens and they cut them open and smeared them into Will's workbooks, hands, clothes. 'Now you'll *have* to wash!' The twins, Hannah and Zoe, hung back and looked miserable; Will didn't blame them. She suspected that they might be very clever. It was dangerous to be clever, at school. And life with Samantha's girls against you was like drowning. Worse, in fact: slower, and more painful.

It was Samantha who showed the others how to widen their nostrils and sniff when Will ran past; they drew back against the walls, whispering and snorting behind curtains of hair; and the teachers called after her from classroom doors, 'You!' Will would have to stop, cold and full of dread on one leg. 'You! What are you doing? Go and put some shoes on please, now. We do *not* go barefoot in the corridors.'

There were the hall monitors, too, who wore badges

on their blazers and shouted, 'Slow down! I'm not going to tell you again, all right?' and, 'You're late, Will,' with depressed sighs; and 'Mop that up, please, Wilhelmina,' and, 'Where's your napkin, Will? Your sleeve is not your napkin.'

At lunch Will took her tray to the toilet block and sat, balancing it on her knees, in the end cubicle. But she couldn't escape dinner, because Mrs Robinson took a register. Rumours went round the Formica-topped dining tables: the new girl spat in your food when you weren't watching. She never changed her underwear. She couldn't read. She couldn't use a toilet. She wiped her hands in her hair. Will, born with bush-hearing, heard them all. But only the last one was true; everyone did, at home. Except the Captain, who was bald; and even he sometimes used his moustache. But the Captain was too precious to talk about.

Instead, she said nothing; and she found, after the first three days of the girls' curiosity and whispering, that she could easily go from the first bell at seven to lights out at nine without speaking a word. Will quickly learnt the value of silence. She did not cry; there was nowhere to go to cry.

At the end of the first week, Miss Blake caught her hiding on the roof of the sports hut. Instead of shouting, she clambered up next to her in her high-heeled shoes.

'Explain it to me, Will.'

'No.' Will shook her head. 'I . . . *sha*. I can't.'

'Try, Will.'

'Thank you, ja. But I can't.' She was struck by how beautiful Miss Blake was, with her large nose and blue eyes. Close up, they were the colour of the African beetles. The climb had left muddy patches on her white shirt.

'Try,' said Miss Blake. 'Sometimes things make more sense when you tell them to other people.'

Will scrubbed at her face with her palms, thereby making her own brand of cement: dust and gravel and tears. 'It's just . . . The bells, ja. The lessons. I can't do the work. And the rules.'

'But we need rules, Will. Can you imagine two hundred girls, and no rules? There'd be murders before fourth period.'

'But it's *them*. The other girls. It's like . . . it's defeat. It's like they've already lost, ja,' she tried not to let her voice grow any louder, any more desperate and angry, 'so they don't *try*, ja, to be good or kind or funny or honest.' Will closed her eyes in a miserable blink.

Miss Blake said nothing, but she sat with Will on the concrete roof, and together they ignored the bell for maths.

CHAPTER EIGHTEEN

Will managed two weeks without changing her clothes or washing her hair. She wanted to keep the smell of Africa as long as she could. But she didn't think it could last; and after lunch on her second Thursday, Mrs Robinson stopped her in the corridor.

'Come with me.' She held out her hand, which Will did not take.

'Your uniform's arrived, at last.' Mrs Robinson was holding a parcel. She looked at Will again – Will, whose head didn't come up to the bookshelf – and frowned worriedly. 'Your guardian didn't give us your height, only your age. You're very small, my dear; I think the skirt will be rather too long.'

Will didn't care. She smiled her secret smile into her chest. The Captain wasn't the sort to know about waist measurements and pleated skirts. She was surprised, now she thought of it, that he even knew how old she was.

'I must say, though –' Mrs Robinson smiled without using her cheek muscles – 'it was a charming letter she wrote, your guardian. She told us all about you, Wilhelmina.'

'What?' Will's head came up with a snap. '*She?*'

'That's right. Mrs Browne. And you *have* had an exciting life, haven't you?'

Will sat silent. Any minute, and this woman would pat her on the head.

'Wilhelmina, my dear, you do have to answer when a teacher speaks to you. It's not optional.'

'Oh.' The thought of the Captain made it hard to speak in a normal voice. She whispered, 'Sorry.'

'And?'

'I – what?'

'I said, you must have had a wonderful life in Zimbabwe?' Mrs Robinson patted her on the head. 'Didn't you?'

'Ja.' Will shied away and gripped handfuls of hair, snuffing their still-African smell.

'What was it like, Wilhelmina?'

'Good.' Will bit her teeth together. 'I loved it. It was good.'

The teacher tried to put an arm round Will's shoulders. They were as stiff and bony as the back of a chair. She sighed.

'Well. Here you are then. Two skirts, four shirts. Try to keep them clean, Wilhelmina. I trust you brought casual clothes for the weekends?'

Will didn't reply; the truth was she had nothing but what she was wearing. But she'd have to face that problem when Saturday came. For now, she climbed into the skirt, shirt, cotton tights. She'd never worn tights, though Cynthia Vincy had drawers full of silky nylon ones which she and Simon had borrowed to carry their stolen oranges. These itched, but they blunted the cold.

The skirt came down past her calves. Will tugged nervously at the too-big waistband. If it fell down during class, and the girls laughed, she'd have no choice but to fight. And she couldn't bear to be kept in at break time, again.

'Try the blazer.'

It was the green of banana leaves, with the school arms embroidered on the pocket. She'd never had anything so smart. She could see, in the mirror, that she looked ugly and strange; thin and pointy, and several sizes too small for her eyes. She tried not to think what her dad would have said. He used to laugh at the smartly dressed girls they passed on their shopping trips, and say, 'Look at that hat! You'd look like a flower in a tea cosy, my wildcat.' And, '*You can't dress fire in a frock.*'

The collar scratched at her neck and made her face itch. That was why, Will told herself angrily, her eyes were watering. The shoes were far too wide and short – 'dancer's feet, you've got,' said Mrs Robinson, and Will bit her lip. 'Elf's feet', her father used to say – so she put her boots on over the tights.

'Very nice,' said Mrs Robinson. 'Very pretty.' She ignored Will's look of incredulity. 'You'll fit in very nicely.'

The girls in the queue for dinner didn't agree.

'You look like you shrunk in the wash!'

'Except you can see she doesn't wash.'

'See? *Smell*, you mean.'

Miss Boniface (whose name, Will thought, did not suit her: she was the science teacher, a stump of a woman with square glasses and large square feet) seemed to agree with that. She caught Will as she ran out of the cafeteria with her plate of food, headed for the toilet block. 'How long have you been here, Will?'

'Two weeks,' Will said. It was Thursday: that made it two weeks exactly.

'And have you washed your hair since you came to Leewood, Will?'

Will looked down at Miss Boniface's feet. 'No.'

'Don't look so sad, my dear! Nobody's going to shout at you. But please ensure you have a bath tonight.' Miss Boniface walked on too soon to hear the laughing that followed Will out of the door.

'Stinking little Silver!'

'Filthy savage.'

They were waiting for her when she reached the

bathroom. Five of them: Samantha, Louisa and Joanna, Bex and Vicky. The bath was filled to the top with water. The room was icy cold.

Will tried to back out again but Louisa had darted behind her, pulled the door shut and locked it.

Samantha said, 'We're come to make sure you wash properly.'

'Go away. Please, ja.'

'No. We're not having you stinking up our bedroom.'

'Filthy little savage.'

'Dirty *midget*.'

They surrounded her in a ring.

Will said, 'You wouldn't. You wouldn't dare.'

'Do you think we're afraid of you? Of a savage with scabby knees?'

'You won't dare. I'll bite.'

Samantha said, 'Get in.' She splashed a handful of water at Will. 'Come on, gypsy. In you get.'

There were too many of them. The room was too small to dodge in. Louisa poked Will in the back. 'Come on. Get in.'

Will whipped round and spat straight in Louisa's face, but the floor was slippery and she skidded and landed, windingly, on her back. The girls pounced. Louisa and Vicky grabbed her arms and Vicky and Bex dug their nails into her legs and they lifted her, fully clothed, into the bathtub. Will tried to bite and kick but it was four against one and her lungs weren't breathing properly in the icy water and she could only spit and gasp, '*Foul.* You're *foul.*'

'She still smells of dirt,' said Louisa.

Samantha pulled open a bottle of shampoo and emptied it over Will's hair and forehead. 'There. Now she smells of coconut and vanilla.' She wiped her hands on her blazer and turned away. 'Let's go.'

Will stopped fighting. She wiped the shampoo out of her eyes. She couldn't see for tears and soapsuds.

Samantha turned at the door. 'And if you so much as think about telling on us, we'll put dog poo in your school bag, OK? Don't forget to empty the bath when you leave. It's in the rules.'

Will waited until their footsteps faded behind them. Then she re-locked the door and stripped off her soaking uniform. She'd brought her shorts and jersey and boots to put on after her bath, along with her long woollen scarf to dry herself with. She didn't have a towel. At home, she dried in the sun by the rock pool. Now she pulled them on, coughing and shivering, and sat down to think.

She must have fallen asleep on the floor of the bathroom, because she awoke to hear the clocks striking across the school. Eleven strokes, and a first that must have woken her up: midnight. The school was silent:

there were only the noises of rain and cold, and further off the roar of the main road. She sniffed at her hair. Africa had gone from it.

She wrapped herself in her scarf and fumbled for the apples she had stored in the too-big pockets of her shorts. She had taken a piece of cheese, too, from the dining hall, but it seemed to have sunk to the bottom of her trousers. Fighting, and crying, had left her famished. Will groped with her bitten nails, sorting through bits of leaf, the woollen gloves from her school uniform, her father's watch, Simon's wildcat, his torch and the Captain's penknife, all glutinously mixed up with chewing gum and pencil shavings and, *yes*, there it was, what felt like the cheese, warm and soft and a little sticky, but definitely edible.

'*Ndatenda hangu*,' Will whispered, '*ja!*', and she felt her chest contract. There were still some good things in this world. Cheese was one of them.

Will pulled at the tangle as carefully as her fingers would allow, but the cold air made her awkward and the Captain's blade bit down into her hand. Will swore and snatched back her fingers, and the knife dropped onto a tile, cracking it down the middle.

The sound rang, agonisingly, down the corridor.

Will held her breath: very distantly, a door opened and closed. A cold drench of dread swept over her. She could still get back to bed, she told herself. She was faster than any teacher. But her legs wouldn't move towards the door. Instead, holding the torch in her teeth, Will scrambled on to the windowsill. It stuck. Will pushed with both hands; she shoved with her shoulders, her knees and feet and head. The window burst open. She hesitated, crouched on the sill. An excited gasping noise came from somewhere nearby: it took Will a few seconds to realise it was her own breath.

The bathrooms were on the first floor; but in the dark, it looked a long way down. The footsteps were approaching the door, now. Will half dropped and half jumped into black air; her left foot caught on the sill and she twisted blindly and landed with a muddy thud on her back.

Her foot was on fire. She curled into a ball, biting on her knuckles and forcing herself not to cry.

'Shut up,' she whispered. 'At least, hey, you can feel it.' That meant her foot was still attached. Shakily, Will got up, pressing herself into the shadow of the wall. As far as she could see in the moonlight she was still in a single piece; she'd lost some of the skin on her knuckles on the way down and she'd bitten her tongue, but she was – astonishingly, gloriously – free. She was ready to shout and shriek and spin and give a wild horseboy whoop when Miss Blake's voice above her head said, 'No one in here. Try the classrooms.'

'I have done, Angela.'

'Try again. I'll look in the arts room.'

Will waited until their noise settled back into silence – then – '*Penga*!' breathed Will. '*Penga*. Have some *sense*, Will.' She could have ruined everything. She swore under her breath – she was so *stupid* – until tears began to prick at her throat and nose, and then she whispered, 'Courage, hey. Truth, ja, and courage.'

She started at a halting run along the main road. A shooting star tore across the sky. Will gave a wordless cough of joy and sped up. The stars danced a war dance overhead. She fell over the pavement and then her own shoes. As she got up, she found to her surprise that she was shaking with cold and pain and nerves. She wrapped the scarf six times round her neck. She pulled her jumper up round her throat. Slowly, with more careful steps, Will walked onwards into the night.

CHAPTER NINETEEN

Will stood on one foot on the pavement, covered in bright sunlight. She could see a gate, and people taking flimsy English money from behind glass screens, and more people than she'd ever seen in her life. Cars – more cars than she'd known existed – drove dizzyingly by. Across the street, red coaches disgorged crowds of men and women, dressed alike in black suits and expressionless faces.

She had walked for five or six hours, using the maps pasted to bus stops to guide her: all she wanted was to keep on in a straight line away from the school. She had lost herself and bumped into things in the dark, and slept for an hour or so on the bench of a bus shelter, and then she had found a file of schoolchildren heading excitedly – where? Somewhere that wasn't school, she could see from their faces – and had followed six steps behind them. And now here she was, standing on one foot, in sharp winter sunlight, under a sign.

London Zoo.

Will was feeling decidedly better – in fact, she realised, quite hugely and wildly better – so much better she had to sing, very softly, behind her hair. She was also feeling achingly hungry. She had eaten the first apple at midnight, and the second at two in the morning, and the third and fourth together with the cheese as an inadequate breakfast when she woke up in the bus shelter. Smells of bacon sandwiches and hot chocolate were rising in puffs from inside the zoo walls. It was easy to slip into the stream of children and in through the gate; easy as working Shumba in with the cattle. Easier, in fact; because she didn't have to lasso any of the children.

Will had never been in a zoo. She knew about them, though, in theory. The idea was a horrible one. There were bars everywhere: it was like Leewood all over again. But the animals, Will grudgingly admitted, looked glossy and properly fed. Which was more than Will was feeling. Her stomach nudged up against her skin again, declaring its emptiness. She shook it off and kept walking, photographing everything with her eyes; there were bushes – I could hide in those, she planned; and benches; those'll be useful later. There was a pen of impala flinging their heads around in the sun. They looked happy; like she and Simon used to be in the early mornings, when the air smelt of bougainvillea and redbush tea. There were vast cages full of multicoloured birds, all of them singing.

The zoo had got some things wrong, though, she thought; no monkey with self-respect would choose a metal climbing frame; and the baboons had the wrong colour of bananas, firm and cartoon-yellow. At home the boons ate them black and spotted, or brown as second best. Once, back at home, a gang of adolescent baboons had snatched a stem of brown bananas, along with a lump of cheese the size of Will's foot and a jug of cider from the veranda table and then had lurched drunkenly around the farmhouse for days, dodging Lazarus's broom and chittering.

Will spent a long time standing in front of the baboons, balling up handfuls of her hair and laughing giddily. When the wind grew too strong, Will worked her way back to the warthogs, which were under cover. She'd always loved warthogs; they were evidence, she reckoned, that the world wasn't always anxious and difficult: it had a sense of humour. She stopped by their enclosure and grinned at their paintbrush tails, flicking to and fro like a pendulum.

'Dad?' A plump little girl a few years younger than Will had stopped and was waving her hamburger at a cluster of them. 'Why are they doing that, Dad? Why are their tails sticking up in the air? Is it like a signal?'

Will waited for the father to answer. He was harassed and tight-lipped and wrestling with a blanket and a toddler in a pushchair. It looked like the toddler was winning.

He said, '*I* don't know, darling. Read the sign.'

Will grinned across the handles of the pushchair. 'It's so they can see each other in the long grass. At home, ja, we had a tame one. He used to do that all the time: he was called Flip.'

The father said, 'At home? Where's that then? Are you from Africa?'

'No!' and Will added, under her breath, 'ach, *booraguma*!' She was so *bad* at this. She had to learn to be always on guard. She shook her head. 'No! No. No, I'm from here.'

'From the zoo?' The girl looked awed.

'No! No, from London, ja.'

'Oh. Me too. Where in London do you live?'

'Just . . . London, ja. Near here.'

'You don't sound like you're from London. You sound foreign.'

'Ja, well.' Will was sick of being told so. 'You sound expensive.'

'Don't be rude, Jennie,' said the girl's father – though it was she, Will, who had been rude, Will knew it, and she frowned at him. Adults didn't understand justice.

Will's frowns were hard to ignore. The man bore it for a few seconds before he looked away. By unlucky chance, his eyes dropped to the space of wind-flayed leg between her shorts and her boots. He frowned. 'Are you sure you're all right? What are your parents thinking, letting you out like that? Not lost, are you?'

'*No.*' Will forced her face out of its scowl. 'I'm with my dad, ja. Sir. He's . . .' The zoo was emptying. There were no unattached adults in sight. 'He's gone to the toilet.'

'Oh dear. Right.' The man looked helpless, and rather nervous of her – of her, and the warthogs, and, in fact, Will thought, of his own children – 'I don't know. Should I be waiting with you until he comes back?'

'No, thank you, ja. I wouldn't like to be a trouble. I should go and look for him, actually . . .' Will began to edge away, taking small silent steps. The man reached out to grab her arm, saying, 'No, wait a second,' – but at that moment the toddler dropped something on the asphalt and let out a bushbaby wail. The girl wailed too. '*Dad!* Tell him off, Dad! That's the second hotdog he's dropped today. He's doing it on purpose!' She had a voice like a mosquito. The warthogs retreated, snorting.

'Don't cry, darling,' The father was red in the face and rather helpless. 'Don't nag, Jennie. We'll buy you another sausage; we'll buy you both another. Come on. Hold on to the buggy, Jen. Less of the animal impressions, Mikey.'

They hurried off; at the corner, the girl turned round and waved at Will. Will waved awkwardly back, with splayed fingers, and waited, aching with suspense, until she could no longer hear their footsteps. Then she snatched up the sausage in its snowy white bun: just as a man in the zoo uniform appeared. His eyes were suspicious.

'I hope you're not planning to eat that, miss.'

Will said, 'Planning to eat it?' She spoke stupidly, like a parrot. If people thought you were stupid, they left you alone.

'It's filthy. Not fit for the animals. Give it here, there's a good girl.'

'No! Thank you. I was just putting it in the bin,' said Will. She was getting the feel of how to lie. She added virtuously, 'I didn't want people to slip in it.'

Because he was still watching, arms folded, Will lowered the bun into one of the black dustbins; but very carefully, onto someone's newspaper, so it wasn't touching the banana skins and cigarette packets; then she carefully waited for him to nod and smile gruffly and walk on; and carefully took it out again and retreated, past the warthogs and past the elephants to the monkey enclosures. There – still carefully – she tucked up her legs on a bench so as to hide the bare skin, and sniffed the sausage deeply, not carefully at all. She inhaled yellow sauce and coughed. Nobody saw: the zoo was almost deserted.

It didn't taste like real sausage; more like tin, and water. But the yellow sauce was delicious – not quite like real mustard; sweeter – and she ate it in four bites and a lick.

As she sat, sucking the sauce out from under her fingernails, a sudden bell sounded. Will felt her heart dilate with brief panic. Somewhere, an invisible giant warned her that the zoo would be closing in quarter of an hour. Would she please collect her personal belongings and make her way to the nearest exit.

What should she do now, she wondered. To give herself time, she hunched smaller and pulled her hair in front of her face. Two girls stopped in front of the monkey enclosure. They were the same age as Will, but wrapped so warmly against the cold they were almost spherical.

'Jess! Look at the one on the top branch – what's it doing?'

'Cleaning itself, obviously.'

'It's not! Look, it's eating.'

'That's what they do. They eat their fleas. And they eat each other's fleas, too.'

'No!'

'They do! It's healthy.'

'Would you eat my fleas?'

'Of course. That's what best friends are for.' The first

girl laughed loudly. Will, watching from her bench, was astonished. Girls, then, weren't all like Samantha. 'Wish we could touch them, though.'

'Wouldn't they bite? You might die of jungle fever.'

'Is there a way in, d'you think?' The girl reached over the barrier and ran her fingers along the wire front of the enclosure.

'Jess! You wouldn't!'

'All right! Calm down. Don't have monkey babies. I'm not going to.'

'What's the word for a monkey-baby, anyway? Are they monkey-cubs?'

'No, cubs is just lions, I think.'

'Mini-monkeys?'

'Monkettes?'

'Let's ask someone – '

They ran – slowly, Will thought, maybe because they were hampered by long coats and scarves tangling under their arms – after a woman in green overalls.

Will waited, careful and wary behind her hair, until they were out of sight. She approached the cage slowly; monkeys got shrieking-scared easily, and these must have had a long day. She stared at the cage front.

Her heart began to tick.

As she stood thinking, statue-still, a boy dragged an old woman and a teenage girl up to the cage; Will ducked behind her hair, and kept studying the wire meshing. It wasn't actually that thick, up close; more like very strong chicken wire. The flickering excitement of a plan began to stir in her stomach and she ran a hand along the wire.

It made the boy look up at her. He stared at Will; at his watch; at Will. Will didn't see; the boy hit his sister with a rolled up comic, saying, 'Lizzie. *Lizzie!*' She brushed him off, so he pulled on the strap of her backpack, whispering, 'Lizzie. *Look*, Liz. That girl's not blinked for two minutes and thirty-eight seconds and –' he looked at his watch again – 'six milliseconds.'

Will heard that; she glared at him and then blinked, as pointedly as she could. Her scowl didn't seem to work on him; he grinned at her. 'New watch for my birthday. It's got an extra-bright night light. It does milliseconds. It can tell the time a mile under water, yeah.'

Will said, 'Oh. How would you get a mile under water?'

'Dunno.' He brushed his fringe out of his eyes to look harder at her. She stared back. His hair looked like he'd cut it himself, in the dark, with the Captain's fish slice, by the light of his extra-bright night light. But his face, underneath it, was good. 'In a submarine, I guess.'

Will said, 'Do you have a submarine?' Perhaps English children were even richer than she'd thought.

'No! Of course not. It was a *joke*, yeah.'

'Oh. Maybe next birthday, ja?'

He laughed. They grinned at each other.

'What's your name? I'm Dan.'

'Will.'

'Seriously? My cousin's called Will. He's a boy.'

'It's a girl's name too.'

'No need to shout. I never said it wasn't. Why aren't you at school?'

'Why aren't you?' Will felt her skin began to tense again.

'Report day. I've been watching you; you're not here with a grown-up.'

She weighed up how much she had to lie to this boy. He had a long, lanky body and a thin, clever face. 'It's a day off, ja.' That was almost true.

He snorted. 'Right. Look,' he checked over his shoulder that the old woman wasn't listening, but she was busy with his sister, 'It's nothing to do with me if you're bunking off; but you should do something about your clothes. Not even tramps wear shorts in February. And your hair.'

'My hair?'

She must have looked stricken – this was the Leewood girls all over again – because he said, 'No! I didn't mean it like that – there's nothing wrong with it – it's nice.' The tips of his ears went red. 'But tie it up, yeah; or put it under a hat. You stick out like a rat in a handbag.'

Will liked that. It was, she thought, the right way to talk. 'We used to say, ja, at home, "like a warthog in a shoe shop".'

He snorted and grinned. His face widened when he smiled, and his ears stuck out like the doors on the Toyota pickup; she liked it: hugely. 'Like a monkey in a tutu,' he said.

'Ja! Ja, ja, like . . .' she wanted something that would make him smile again . . . 'a giraffe on a swing set.'

'Like a wildcat in a classroom,' he said. Will choked and stared, suddenly frightened and suspicious. He said, 'What?'

'Nothing . . . no, nothing.'

'Right,' he said. His grandmother was smiling and tapping her watch. 'Look, I've got to go. You – you do have food, yeah? Dinner money?'

'Food?' Will tried, and failed, to look like someone with a well-stocked fridge in tow.

'Yeah, food. You know – edible things? Stuff that makes you grow? Wait; don't go. I've got a Mars. Here. You can have half of it.' He split it in two; and then his own half again, stickily. 'Wait; you can have three-quarters. And here – take this,' he tore his comic down the centre fold. 'You can have the first half of this. I've read the first half anyway.'

His grandmother tapped him on the shoulder.

'Daniel, love. We'll miss the bus. Say goodbye to your friend.'

Will was surprised by how sharply it hurt her chest to see him go. She wished, for perhaps the nine hundred and ninety-ninth time, that Leewood hadn't been an all-girls school.

There were no humans in sight now; only the orang-utan watching with interest, and a baboon scratching its ankle, and the two monkeys. The heaps of straw in the monkey cage looked warm and soft (though straw wasn't ever as soft as it looked; Will knew that from nights with the horses) and it smelt like home.

Will pulled off her gloves with her teeth and shoved them into her pocket. She spat on her hands and, with a scrabbling kick, pulled herself high up and over the barrier. She checked again over her shoulder; all was clear. The wire front of the cage was easy to climb – it was the same stuff the Captain used to protect his goats from the *nzunas* and jackals – but here the roof was wire as well, whereas the Captain's was corrugated iron. At the top Will crouched and pulled out her knife. She'd found it rusting in a stash of tools by the East edge of the farm, and the secateurs on it were sharp, designed to cut through meat and bone. All the same, she was astonished at how easy it was to cut a hole in the wire as wide as her shoulders – she thought, *good thing I'm so small, after all* – and even as she was shivering with excitement she remembered to wrap her hands in her scarf before she gripped the rough edge she'd made. Through the scarf she felt the barbed edges cut into her palms. She bit down on her lips, and made no noise.

With both hands gripping the rough edge of the hole, Will lowered her legs into the cage. She kicked off her boots and – this was harder – her socks. They dropped down into the cage and bounced into the straw. Will swung her legs up and gripped at the wire with her toes and hung there for a second, upside-down-on-all-fours, with everything but her head inside the cage. Then she had to stop for a second to laugh, silently and wildly. She bit her tongue to stop herself. '*Concentrate*, hey.'

Will edged towards the wire front of the cage and began to inch down it. It was slow, and painful, with every finger in a separate hole, straining with her own weight and cutting into slices on the wire edge. And then Will felt her stomach lurch, before her head knew why; and then she recognised the thump of footsteps, and she was still only halfway to the ground. She sped up, sliding and bending her fingers backwards, and then suddenly everything was upside-down and blurred and black and a monkey was screaming, and she was tumbling down amongst the straw. She landed badly, on one knee, and all the air coughed out of her lungs. Unable to breathe and blind and heaving, by instinct she found she was scrabbling into the straw and tucking her head between her knees just in time to hear a man's voice say, 'What's all this, eh? What's going on here?'

Will waited. She bit her lip and didn't answer: he might not be talking to her. His voice had that sticky lilt that people used in this country for babies and animals.

The voice said again: 'What's all the ruckus, Wilbur, lad? Did someone feed you Coke again, Wilbur? Did they give you mustard?'

A second voice said, 'Bloody kids. Can't they read the sign? *Do not feed the animals*.'

'Probably not. Illiterate little blighters.' And there was laughter.

'Come on. Sandra's promised to buy us a pint.'

The steps passed on, and the lights over the Refreshment kiosk went out. The zoo was filled with darkness; and the solid murmur of a hundred animals; and Will's audible heart.

CHAPTER TWENTY

It was one of the happiest nights of Will's life.

As she unclenched her fingers from around her ankles there was a ripple in the straw behind her. A hand – a hand like a baby's fist, but with sharp nails and black fur – tugged at her hair. Another fastened on her shoulder. Over her shoulder, a beautiful black face appeared.

Will breathed, '*Oh . . .*' and then, '*Oh . . .*'

The monkey licked her eyelashes.

There weren't words.

It didn't take long to explore the whole cage, though it was large enough. There were two monkeys, and a tyre swing, a climbing frame, and her. The larger monkey (Will guessed it must be Wilbur – though it seemed far too formal a name for a monkey. But then, Will was an odd name for a girl, they said at school) squatted up on a branch in a corner, unsure and resentful of the enormous intruder. Will gave him as much space as she could: an angry monkey, she knew, wasn't a good sleeping companion. She and Simon both had scars to prove it.

But the other monkey was small, with arms as thin as the tines of forks, and he clung to Will's neck and arms when she stood up. He breathed love into her ears, and nibbled her eyebrows and tried to lick the inside of her nose.

'Hey!' whispered Will. 'Hey-hey . . . Hush, beauty . . . Oi oi oi. If I wanted to fight I'd have stayed outside, my dear. Hush, ja? Hush, beauty.'

Will found her torch and wrapped her hair over it to dim the light, and then moved very slowly, very silently across every inch of the floor, looking for food. She didn't know what zoos thought monkeys ate; she hoped for bread, and apples and carrots, sweet corn and cheese. Half an hour of searching produced a handful of sunflower seeds, half a mango and a dusty banana. It was black, and flies buzzed around it, but Will felt soft and exhausted with hunger.

As soon as she sat back against the wall, the monkey reached into her lap and fumbled at the banana.

'Hey! *Sha*, hey!' she whispered, 'I gave you some of my Mars bar, remember?' The monkey patted Will's mouth with a tiny fist. She gave him the last quarter, and half the skin to lick.

Will piled straw into a heap in the far corner of the enclosure, where she thought she should be shielded from passing keepers by the climbing frame. She made a ball of the softer hay and wrapped her scarf round it for a pillow. She stuffed more into her boots, her shorts, and between her T-shirt and jumper. Steadily, she grew warmer. She blew on her hands. Across the zoo, night birds sang into the stars.

Will lay down, and the monkey nuzzled its face into her neck. Its eyelids fluttered like black moths. Will breathed in its living-happiness animal smell. She had forgotten, too easily, how beautiful the world was.

Will woke up with straw in her ears and mouth. Wherever she was was warm and dark and smelt familiar, but her memory was a great throbbing blankness. Then a hand reached out and tugged at her hair. Will pushed it away. The hand grasped her ear, and Will opened her eyes.

The hand was attached to an arm, which was in turn attached to a pair of black eyes and a velvet mouth and a tail as long as Will's spine.

Will felt recollection swoop over her, and with the happiness of it, there was a shiver of fear.

She whispered to herself, *penga*, and then, 'Idiot, *idiot*.' She'd forgotten the desperate importance of staying free. Or rather – she admitted it grudgingly – she hadn't forgotten; she just hadn't wanted to remember. There was a difference.

The monkey wrapped itself round Will's chest. She buried her head in his long silky hair. She breathed his delicate earthy smell, and he chattered and pulled at her ears, settling himself more comfortably in her arms.

With the sort of flashes of genius that come at two o'clock in the morning, Will had laid plans to live in the zoo. She would sleep with her monkey, here, under cover of straw, and maybe have breakfast with the gorillas – because she reckoned they'd get the best food, being largest – and then she could spend the rest of the days standing by the warthogs, and stealing food from the Refreshment kiosk, and dodging the zoo keepers.

In the dawning light, and the cold mean drizzle that blew in through the wire, Will knew it was mad and impossible. There were thousands of people working here, and security cameras everywhere, and perhaps police looking for her. 'Not sensible, Will Silver,' she said. She sighed. 'England is the home of common sense.'

The monkey chattered, agreed. She rubbed its fur between her fingers. It was so smooth it felt wet. 'What do you think, hey? Ja? Shall I take you with me?' It would be so good to have a friend again. She couldn't have one at the school; because at school, all the good bits of her – the tree-climbing-sunlit-jumping-catapulting parts – were useless. They thought she was boring. 'They hate me.' But taking the monkey would be impossible. One girl – especially a small one: a *midget-savage*, they said – could, she hoped, hide fairly easily. One girl and a hungry monkey, less so.

She untwined his arms from around her neck. He re-twined them. Will kissed the monkey's eyes and nose; then she pulled the lace out of one boot and tied his back paw to the far wall. It wouldn't hold for more than five minutes, but it might be enough to stop him following her. Will would need her toes to climb, so she tied her boots to her belt loop with the remaining shoelace.

Will turned to the wire, and gave it a tug. The morning was still quite dark. She should be able to get out the way she'd come if she went right now, before the zoo opened, right this minute, though it wouldn't be as easy; her ankle had begun to swell and her arms ached. And *oh*, it was so hard to force her bruised fingers to grab and pull and lift. She'd never felt so stiff, or so tired.

To distract herself from the terror of falling, Will tried to make plans. Planning whilst hanging upside-down by your fingers and toes from a wire cage is difficult, but not impossible. The first problem was where she should run to. In the centre of London there would be parks, she knew from the girls at school; and museums where you could sit for free. Above all, there would be rich people. Will squeezed herself through the hole in the roof, moaning with the effort. If you needed meat, you went to watering holes or the grasslands: where animals congregated. So if you needed money, you went where the rich people came in herds. And that was London.

Will dropped to the ground in front of the barrier, trying and failing to land silently. Her plan made sense.

CHAPTER TWENTY-ONE

Halfway along the first road she walked down, Will found an abandoned sleeping bag and half a can of something. She sniffed it: it was some kind of beer. She hadn't had a drink since the water from the taps in the zoo toilets yesterday. She sipped it, and then spat it out immediately. It tasted like pond water. Will tipped it down the drain and wiped her mouth on her hair. She'd rather be thirsty than drink that, she thought.

Two hours later, helplessly lost, Will was starting to regret her decision. Her throat was aching and rough, and she felt her stomach gurgling more urgently. The beer, though, had given her an idea: if people threw away whole cans of drink, what else would the world have left out for her? At the next dustbin she came across, Will she stopped and checked over her shoulder. Nobody was watching her.

The dustbin was full of cigarette butts and plastic bags, mostly, but beneath them was a crisp packet, Salt and Vinegar, with broken crisp-shards in the bottom corners. Will fished it out – it looked fairly clean – and was just running her finger around the inside and luxuriously licking off the fragments when a round-faced boy grabbed at his father and cried, 'Dad! *Dad*! Look! That girl's eating *rubbish*!'

Will froze with her tongue still poking out. The boy's father made a grab at her. She tugged and squirmed, gasping, 'Let me *go*,' and buried her teeth in his hand. He was shouting – 'Come back! I'm trying to *help*!' – but Will, shivering with horror, tore through a group of gaping tourists and fled. She didn't stop until she had counted to three hundred: long after footsteps had ceased to pursue her.

The hunger was growing more painful. Will swung her arms to propel herself onwards. The second good dustbin she found was ten minutes on, down an alley, as narrow as a bush-path from home, flanked by sky-high buildings and deserted except for a man sleeping in a doorway. It smelt of urine and she recognised the pungent, rank bitterness of rats.

Will pushed her hair behind her ears. She squared her shoulders; she whispered a prayer. She crossed her fingers – and then uncrossed them, because she couldn't rummage using only her thumbs. The dustbin was spilling over with tin cans, and scraps of cigarettes. Her hand closed on something promising and hard: the last centimetre of a chocolate bar; someone must have been on a diet, she thought. She'd never heard of diets until she came to England. She ate it, telling herself firmly it was no different to stealing sugar from the kitchens, or fruit from the compost bin, which she'd done almost every day at the farm. If she was caught her father swiped at her legs with his stick and laughed. Will shivered again; this time not with cold.

Will forced herself to concentrate. She reckoned she had to eat properly, immediately, or faint into that yellow puddle at her feet. She picked out the crusts of a sandwich. The teeth marks were still on them. They weren't mouldy; but memories of the girls at school – what they'd say – cut at her heart. *Filthy savage*, she thought. And *dirty little animal*.

Footsteps approached. Instinctively, Will dropped down behind the bin. Don't shiver; she told herself. Don't move. Try to imitate a pavement. She heard the thump of something heavy against the sides of the dustbin and footsteps receding.

Will crouched on the pavement long after they'd passed. Her legs ached too much to stand and her veins were full of icy water. She thought, *come on, chook*. Her father would have said that – and, *courage, hey*. Will pulled herself up using the rim of the bin and lifted out a polystyrene carton with careful hands. Inside it was a mountain of potato chips, lagooned in a sort of red sauce, barely touched and still hot.

Dizzy with her luck – and with hunger too, probably – Will threw back the crusts and tucked up her knees on a doorstep to eat her prize. The rain began to fall in muddy curtains, soaking her hair, but the warmth from the chips was like a kiss. Potatoes, Will reckoned, solved a lot of problems.

When Will rounded a corner just as evening fell and saw a sign to the park, the surge of joy was so great she had to stop and clutch at her stomach. It was stronger even than the day she'd first ridden Shumba. It was like a blast of warmth to her toes: like new courage. The big clever busy city continued to sweep past her, roaring and spluttering and frowning and pushing. But, Will reminded herself, she was clever too.

The road to the park gates (Hyde Park, a sign said, and she saw that as a good omen: hide was exactly what she needed to do now; hide, plan, run, in that order) was long. Will tried to keep herself to a slow jog, with a hop in it every other step to protect her ankle.

The air was less sharp and cold than yesterday, but windier, which Will liked. The wind was turning umbrellas inside out and blowing her hair wildly across her face, and was loud enough to drown the music of a man playing a violin in the street until she was almost standing on him. She was enchanted; not just by the music, which was dragonfly-quick, but by the people who dropped coins into his hat. Will retreated to a safe distance and crouched to watch. At home, nobody danced or sang for money. They did it because there was too much happiness in their chests; or because they were angry, or bored. It was like breathing. It had never occurred to her that dancing and singing could be sold. But it looked a glorious idea.

She thought, *If I had a hat* . . . But possibly winter clothes in general would work? Will smoothed out her scarf on the pavement and stood behind it. She needed a sign, really, and she should put money in it, to show people what she wanted them to do, but she had no money. She found a bottle cap instead, and a round thin pebble, and a ring-pull from a beer can.

Will squatted against a lamppost to tie her trailing lace, checked left and right for police, and kicked her legs up into a handstand. It wasn't easy: at home she was always barefoot, but now her heavy boots wobbled in the air. They made gravity harder to measure. She could usually hold it for four or five minutes, but her jersey was slipping down over her eyes so that her stomach was bare to the wind and she couldn't see if people were stopping to look. She didn't hear the chink of money.

Will twisted upright. Nothing; not half a dollar (no, she corrected herself; pound). She tucked her jersey into her shorts and spat on her hands. She had no elastic for her hair, but there were a couple of well-shaped twigs nearby. She held it for longer this time; maybe two minutes, she thought, before an upside-down voice said, 'My dear! You're creating an obstruction.'

Will struggled upright. A crowd of boys were watching her, blocking the path of a wrinkled woman with a shopping bag on wheels.

Will blushed. She whispered, 'Sorry! Sorry, ja,' and pressed herself against the wall, smiling her polite-to-visitors to smile. The boys retreated a few steps and jeered. Will ignored them; they were hyenas, she thought. She whispered it: *Hyenas*. Hyenas were the one animal Will didn't like. They smelt disgusting, she thought, like wet straw and old meat. She clarified out loud: 'Hyenas. Not those boys.' But the boys smelt too: of old cigarette smoke and greasy armpits.

Will looked away from them, fixing her eyes on the sky instead. She tipped backward into a bridge shape, and walked to and fro like a crab behind her scarf. The concrete was icy and she could see, upside-down, that her fingers were turning blue. Nobody put money in her scarf. Apparently handstands and bridges did not impress English people.

Will got up again. Shivering in the drizzle she did two messy back flips; but she had never tried on a pavement and her wrists smarted sharply, and on the third she landed with one palm in broken glass. A fat woman stared and made as if to stop; Will bit down on her sleeve, determined not to cry out.

'What are you *doing*?' Will whispered. The wind drowned her voice, which meant she was safe to say it out loud, 'Be careful. Have some *sense*, Will Silver. England is the land of common sense, hey.' A hospital would send her straight back to Leewood, and Will felt her skin tighten with the horror of the thought. Will resolutely picked out the few shards, and wrapped her hand in her sock (she'd lost both gloves somewhere between yesterday and today) and stood on her head.

Upside down and in the wind, Will sang.

She sang 'Nkosi sikelele Africa', the South African anthem, which her father had taught her as soon as she could talk because it was so beautiful and sounded, he said, like impala drinking at a waterhole; and then the English national anthem, though she wasn't quite sure of the words after the first line and had to la-la the last bits. An upside-down woman glared at her, with frown marks like a railway line, and Will stopped. It might, for all she knew, be heresy. She remembered, suddenly, the songs she and Simon sang at night by the fires.

'Inkie Pinkie Ponkie, Ayeh!' Will called into the wind. Nobody stopped. Will sang louder,

'Father bought a donkey, Ayeh!

'Donkey died, Father cried,

'Inkie Pinkie Ponkie, Ayeh!'

Will saw a cluster of upside-down shoes stop in front of her, and the click of cameras, and quick laughing talk in a foreign language. Chinese, perhaps, she thought. Will sang louder. Squinting, upside-down, she saw a handful of copper coins drop onto her scarf; and then foreign female laughter, and then a proper hail-storm of coins. Some of them, she thought, were those chunky little English pound coins.

'Thank you! Thank you, hey!' Upside-down, Will laughed with the triumph and kicked her legs in the air, until her shirt fell back over her eyes. She gurgled and panted and tried to breathe through the cloth, and then choked and toppled over sideways and leapt up, her heart turning victorious somersaults.

There was a scuffling sound as she stood up, and pounding feet. Will brushed her hair out of her eyes. Her scarf and money had gone.

The gang of boys were sprinting down the road towards the park gates.

It was hard; it was too hard not to cry. Will hurled herself after them, shaking and sobbing, and then tripping and grazing her good knee. They hadn't seen her coming; they were clustered under a tree, shoving and grabbing at the largest boy. He held both hands over his head, out of their reach.

'You've got it, haven't you?' said Will. She hadn't seen their faces: she couldn't be sure it was them. Will bit the inside of her cheeks. Nothing was certain in England. That was the problem. Everything was unfamiliar; even *boys*.

'You've got it.'

The largest boy had spots, and his lip curled up under his nose with distaste. 'Wha'? Got wha'?'

'My scarf. It's *mine*. It's from my farm, ja. It was my dad's. You've got my scarf and my money.' She felt limp and helpless. 'You *took* it.' Justice was only easy in books. '*Please*.' She didn't know what else to say.

'We done nuffin'. Sod off.' The curled lip advanced on her. Will backed away a step.

'Yeah, sod off.' The other boys stepped closer.

'I said *please*.'

The boys swore. 'Bugger off, yeah?' One picked up a stick and waved it at her, as though she were a dog.

'Get lost, all right?' The boys – six or seven of them, years older than her, at least two heads taller – cracked their knuckles. Will stared. Cracking your knuckles to fight: surely only cretins did that. She stopped backing.

'I need it, ja.' She felt her knees and elbows lock themselves, ready. 'This isn't a game. Please. Give it back.'

'Don't know what you're talking about.' They were laughing.

'Oh! No, wait, guys! I think I know what the little gypsy means.' One of them – the boy with a neck thicker than Will's waist, a buffalo of a boy – put his hand in his pocket and pulled out a handful of pound coins. He wafted them under her nose. 'Was this what you was talking about?'

'Yes!' Will held out her hand. 'That's mine.'

'Mine now, though, isn't it? It's finders keepers, yeah. We're teaching you a lesson, yeah? Look after what you got.'

Will's body convulsed with anger and she grabbed at his arm. She never touched strangers. He felt clammy and cold. '*Please*, ja. Please.'

The wind was picking up again and the boys were shouting over it, mimicking her voice, 'Please! Yarr! *Pretty* please?'

Will tightened her grip on his wrist – '*Please*!' and squeezed in earnest, vicious, trying to stop the blood. '*Please*.'

'Get *off* me!' he said, and he drove his elbow hard into her face.

Will was stunned for a second. The world darkened and buzzed. She swayed. Then every stored-up ounce of misery and fury, every locked-up scream since her father's death exploded, fire-hot, inside her chest, and she threw herself at him, roaring and weeping rough sobs, hammering with her fists, her head, her knees. Some of the other boys made grabs at her, and the fat boy bellowed and thrashed, backing away into two of his gang and collapsing into a kicking, spitting heap. 'Get her *off*!'

Will had never fought like this. Every unswung punch and unspat spit of the last two weeks boiled up inside her. She kicked one boy in the kneecap; and found the face of another under her right hand and wrenched upwards into his nostrils with two fingers. He shrieked. The others stopped laughing, froze, stared. The one who had had hold of her hair slowly unclenched his fist.

Will pushed him away and got up on shaky legs. 'Give it to me. I need it.'

The largest boy stared. 'God! You little *savage*!' He threw the money and scarf on the grass. He tried to spit on them, but Will could see his mouth was dry and he could only dribble. He edged away from her. His face was bleeding. 'You *little* . . .'

'Come on, Rob.'

'You little . . . savage. Are you crazy?' Still staring, still backing away, the boys swore at her, spat on the ground. Two kicked stones at her head. Will ducked the first one and caught the second in two fingers of her unbandaged hand – it was instinctive, she couldn't think in a straight line, let alone see in one. She let it drop to the ground.

'Bloody *hell*!' The girl was obviously abnormal. She still hadn't blinked. The boys turned, and ran.

'*Sha*,' Will whispered. She dropped to the ground against the tree and hugged her chest, waiting for the shaking in her fingers to calm. '*Sha*.' Under her hands,

167

her heart was rattling around like a cutlery drawer in an earthquake. She spoke to an imaginary Simon. '*Sha*, hey?' She hadn't known she could fight like that.

But she hadn't known she could lie, either. She hadn't known she could hate so many people. She was learning a lot of things. The wind blew her hair into her mouth and she spat it out angrily.

With her good hand, Will counted out the money, making piles of the coins: pounds, fifties, twenties, tens. There was a mound of coppers. Together she had more than eight English pounds. That was a start. Not enough, though, for a bed in a hotel, because the girls at school said those cost hundreds, even thousands. That was another thing to hate about England; Will stuffed the coins deep in her pocket. Nothing was free, here.

Perhaps she could sleep here, on the grass, she told herself. It was soft and smelt sweet. But she was muddy enough already; and the muddier you were the more grown-ups stared. And, she thought, there was always the chance the boys would come back. She couldn't bear to be ambushed.

A flurry of wind and falling leaves made her look up. The tree she was leaning against was a great, generous spreading giant – like a baobab at home, but thinner, and with leaves – and the branches were thick. They would be protection from the wind, as well as concealment.

Will hauled herself to her feet. It was dusk already

– daylight seemed an endangered species, here – but not too dark to see footholds in the bark. There was a place, maybe ten feet up, where two branches slotted into the trunk at right angles to it, like the slats in the seat of a chair. She settled herself astride them, with her back against the trunk. Experimentally, Will closed her eyes. It was as firm as a horse, and she'd often fallen asleep on Shumba's wide back; but if she fell off Shumba, it was only sixteen hands to the ground.

Will fumbled with her scarf, keeping one hand firmly on a branch level with her chin. By slow inchings, she found she could work the scarf once round the trunk, then loop it round her waist like a belt, twist it, and then once round the trunk again, tying the ends tightly in a triple knot. It was just long enough. She gave it a tug. It neither loosened nor tightened; that, her father used to say, was the sign of a good knot. Oddly, the thought of him hurt a little less than it had before: and instead of freezing her stomach, it warmed her cheeks. Experimentally, she leaned back over the edge. The scarf stretched, but held her weight.

Will tucked her chin between her knees for warmth, and hid her eyes in the crook of her elbow. Tied tight to the trunk, breathing in bark and the deep rough air, Will fell asleep. Her dreams were of girls with heavy boots, dancing with the wind.

CHAPTER TWENTY-TWO

Will's muscles must have woken before she did, because she came to consciousness with her arms and legs tense and braced against something cold and wet and rough. Her head felt heavy and sodden, full of uncooked dough. Birds were singing very close by; oddly close; right up against her face, it felt. Will opened her eyes. She was wedged in the branches of a tree. Sudden fear and dizziness and hunger swooped over her and she was sick, over the edge of the branch, before she'd fully woken up.

Groggily, she wiped her mouth and spat. She must have slept longer than she planned, because the sun was rising and already there were people running through the park dressed in odd plastic-looking clothing. It wasn't raining – for a miracle, Will thought, and smiled at the sky.

Will worked herself more securely astride her branch. The wind was blowing and making the branches shake; but if the tree worked in the same way as the ones at home, she was safe enough. She leant against the trunk and steadied herself with her good hand; she kept the other free, to list her options on her fingers. Above anything else, she needed money. She had eight pounds and ninety-four pence. That wouldn't last long. For an aeroplane ticket, she'd need more than eight pounds. How did you get that sort of money? Will put up one finger; she could steal – from people, or, better, from shops – she imagined she'd be good at it. But that wasn't courage: stealing, her father said, was for people with tin hearts and snotty souls. She could get a job, perhaps. Will added another finger. What job? There were no horses in London, so she couldn't be a horseboy. People didn't get paid for the things she was good at: she could run a mile without stopping, and shoot an air rifle, and put both ankles behind her neck, but she wasn't sure that made her very employable. Lastly – Will's hand made a fist and she bit at the knuckle – she could beg.

Will knew about begging. Young girls with babies tied to their backs begged in the streets of Harare. Her father took pockets of change when he went into town, and legs of ostrich and impala wrapped for them in grease-proof paper. On her shopping trip Cynthia Vincy had waved them away like they were mosquitoes.

Will bit down on her scarf to stop her teeth chattering. Cynthia had told her (several times; had never stopped telling her, in fact) that an aeroplane ticket cost a thousand American dollars. That was five hundred English dollars (or, *no*, Will corrected herself: *pounds*). If she earned one dollar – one *pound* – a day, she could fly back in five hundred days. There were three hundred and sixty five days in a year: that made a year and a half. If she earned *five* pounds a day, it would take (Will squinted up at the leaves and counted on her fingers) four months. Ten pounds a day would be two months. Twenty pounds a day would mean she had enough to go home in one month. A month was only thirty days. She whispered, *'courage, chook,'* and her heart beat back at her confidently. She could do thirty days.

The tree top above her swooped – like a hawk in the wind, she thought – and she caught hold of the trunk with her other hand and waited for the leaves to calm, wincing at the cuts under her bandage-sock. Thirty days; *I can do that*, she told herself: live in this tree at night, and beg every day; find matches for a fire (could you light a fire in a tree? She'd never heard of anyone doing it; but that didn't mean it couldn't be done) and then when the time came she wouldn't tell anyone; she'd just get on a plane, and then hitch from the airport to central Harare, and from there the bus to Mutare, and a day's run to Two Tree Hill, and it didn't matter who owned the farm now, even if it was the Madisons, because Simon would still be there, and Tedias and Lazarus. She could build a hut, and hunt rock-rabbit, and make stew out of corn and cabbage leaves. It would take time, but she'd have time, with no school bells cutting up the days into miserable chunks, and there would be fruit to eat and sunshine and Kezia. Kez would be old enough to train properly. That would be worth begging for, she thought.

The tree shook again, and leaves dropped into her face and bark-dust blew into her eyes. Will found she went on shaking after it had stilled; that meant she needed to eat soon. And it was getting light. She blew on her hands and dropped to the ground. Her boots squelched and her ankle jarred with every step but she could walk – and run, she thought, if she needed to – and she was still free. So it was three parts excitement to one part fear.

Will headed east out of the park. She needed a train station, or a museum, or a busy street; somewhere where she wouldn't stick out. She had no idea where the English kept their train stations, but the sun rose in the east, and it seemed a more hopeful direction than any other.

For begging, women would be best, she decided; they walked slower than the men (because of those shoes on tiny stilts, she thought, and grinned: she and Simon had laughed at Cynthia Vincy's shoes, and they'd hidden the worst pair – made from *chameleon* skin, as though Miss Vincy didn't know how slow and funny and wise chameleons were – in the compost heap) and most women she saw carried bags that might be full of loose change. She couldn't see where men would keep their coins, and credit cards would be no good.

Will walked on, trying not to limp, until she found a street where everyone shone with money. Their hair glistened. The women tack-tacked on high heels. The men weren't as strong as her father, but sleeker: more dangerous. Will wrinkled her nose at them, and hugged herself until the shudder in her chest abated.

Will ran her fingers through her hair. She had no way of knowing how she looked: dirty, she imagined, and bruised. The cold night had made her sniff, and she had a little moustache made of snot and wind. Still, she could smile; she'd been told she had a good smile, and she would choose the passers-by with soft, gentle faces.

Will's first three attempts failed; she wasn't loud enough, too small, and they swept by before she got beyond the 'ex' of 'excuse me'.

But the fourth woman stopped and smiled. 'Yes, love?'

'Excuse me, ma'am,' said Will again. 'Could you spare some change?' It was what she'd heard the men in doorways saying. This was the one place, she reckoned, where it was important to fit in.

'Have you lost your mum, sweetie?' The woman smiled. It was a very kind smile.

'No.' That was true. 'I know where she is. Could you spare some change?'

'How old are you, love? You can't be more than eight.'

Will set her teeth. She repeated, 'Could you spare some change, ma'am? I need to get home.'

'Of course you do, poppet.' She laid a hand on Will's shoulder. 'Why don't you come with me? Come on. You look frozen to death. We'll take you somewhere safe.'

When they said *safe* they meant *trapped*. Will flinched away. Something in the movement – something unEnglish, Will supposed; *feral* they said at school – made the woman tighten her grip and look closer at Will's face.

'Wait a minute, pet. You're not that girl – in the paper? I thought I recognised – Good *God*! You are! – and there was something about a zoo –' Will was suddenly conscious of the straw in her hair, and the smell of animal – 'and half the police force out looking. What's your name, dear?'

Her hold on Will's hood was firm and excited. Will said, 'Samantha Ronald.'

'Samantha? No – I'm sure that wasn't the name.'

'It's Samantha, ja!'

The woman's eyes narrowed. 'What was that? Are you foreign, dear?'

'*No*,' said Will. That at least was true. She was just in the wrong country.

'Well. Why don't we take you somewhere warm?' The woman was trying to catch the eye of a policeman. The policeman, to Will's relief, was trying in turn to catch the eye of a pretty blonde girl swishing down the street. 'Why don't we just —'

The hood was attached to the jersey with loose wool stitches. Will had put them in herself when the first ones unravelled, and she'd been impatient, and Simon had been whistling at her from the stables: *shameful and slipshod*, Cynthia Vincy had called it. Will remembered it, and was desperately glad; she gave a hiss and a spit to make the woman step back; and then she jerked sideways and there was a ripping and a shout and she was away, running hard, weaving through herds of city people. A few turned at the woman's cry of 'Stop her! Stop that little girl!' and caught at her scarf and flying hair, but Will was fast and desperate. The wind got into her eyes and she heard people cry and shriek in outrage as she crashed into them and rebounded and all she could do was keep going. Her mind was blank save two words: *run*; and *police*.

Will couldn't look round until she'd counted twenty streets between her and the woman and then she twisted to check. Nobody was chasing her. She collapsed, coughing, against a wall, with a stitch biting at her side and a dry mouth. People passed by with smart leather boxes on handles and flimsy cups of coffee, hailing black bubble-shaped cars. Will retched, and choked. Slowly, her breath returned, though her hands wouldn't stop quivering.

A man at a bus stop stood up to stare better. 'Are you all right, down there? What are you doing?'

Will flushed, and she felt her stomach tighten again. 'Nothing. Just sitting.'

He frowned, 'Wait a moment. Aren't you –?'

Will jumped up, shaking her head and trying to smile reassuringly. '*No*. No Engleesh. French.'

He said, 'What? What are you on about? No, wait: come here . . .' he was fumbling with his paper, tapping the print on the third page. 'Isn't this –'

'I not speak Eenglish, ja.' Scowling, Will backed away, waiting to see if he would shrug and turn away. At that moment a bus arrived, and he started fumbling in his pockets for his wallet. Will judged it was safe to turn her back and limp on. Now she was going slower, Will noticed that the people passing, wrapped in their coats and hats and hoods, were staring at her bare knees; so as soon as she came to the open doors of a museum, she veered gratefully in. She needed a dark corner in which to sit, and breathe, and think.

CHAPTER TWENTY-THREE

The museum was full of cabinets displaying jewellery and watches and clothes on silver hangers. The hangers looked like solid silver, and that was extraordinary; they were marvellously pretty. She'd made all the coat hangers at home herself, out of garden wire or wood. Will shook off her longing to touch the clothes – you didn't touch in museums, that was the *point* – and pulled herself up some stairs. Her feet were throbbing, and she felt suddenly small and angular under the high ceilings. She put out a finger and touched the banister: it was real silver, with a real silver smell.

At the top, Will found a great room that was empty; just silent chandeliers and more exhibits of jewellery. She sank to the floor in a corner; it wasn't a *dark* corner, because the whole museum was delicately and femininely lit, but it was darker than the rest, and her legs desperately needed to curl up for a few moments. She tucked her knees under her jumper and tore at a thumbnail.

So – Will clenched her eyes shut and bit the nail off

her middle finger – the police were looking for her. Begging had failed. (Secretly, she was glad about that. Wildcats do not beg.) What now?

The carpet was thick and wonderfully soft, and she felt as though she'd barely slept in the tree, and it was so *warm*; the warmest she'd been since the farm . . . Will tried to arrange her thoughts into tidy piles, but they kept floating away, out of reach . . .

Will woke up to a woman standing over her saying, 'Can I assist you, miss?'

The woman's expression was less courteous than her words. 'Miss?' she repeated. She addressed the leaves and mud stuck to Will's knees.

Will blinked. 'I – please –'

'Are you here with someone?'

'I . . . ja. I –.' Will scrubbed at her left eye.

'Really?'

'Ja! Yes. They're . . . they're over there –'

'Where?'

'That man – in black –' She pointed at a figure across the room; a dark motionless back.

'The *mannequin*?' The woman's voice curled like a sneer.

'No! No, just over there . . .'

'I *see*. Very good.' Her face said the exact opposite. 'I think you'll have to come with me.'

'*No*! He must have gone round the corner.' Will

worked her face into the shape of a Leewood girl. She flared her nostrils haughtily. 'I swear, ja,' She could see her reflection in one of the long mirrors: she looked like a princess with a mouth ulcer, her father would have said.

The woman blinked. She looked unnerved. But she didn't leave. 'I think you will have to come with me, miss, and we will find a telephone. *Immediately*, please.'

'We will *not*.' Will could feel her lips moving; but the voice that came out was Samantha's. 'Thank you. I'd like to be left alone. My father is a very rich man. He won't like it if I say you bullied me.' Will turned on her filthy boot and stalked – every inch of her a Leewood girl – around two corners, past a table of leather bags, and out of the woman's sight: and then Will ran. She darted past rows and rows of hats and jewels, winding in and out of glass cases, searching feverishly for the stairs. She found some by an exhibit of jewels and hurtled down them. She was ten steps down before she realised in horror that they were moving, carrying her back *up*, towards the woman who was waiting with crossed arms and a fixed stare at the top. Panicking and breathless, Will half leapt, half tripped the rest of the way, dodging shouts and screams. She tore past three cash registers and the rustle of carrier bags, and out.

She stared. '*Oh*.' Not a museum, then. The sign above the building said 'Harrods'. Suddenly the doors swished, and the woman stepped out. Will turned and ran.

Sixteen streets away, Will stopped, gasping, and shook out her arms and legs. But it did nothing to dispel the tense tightness in her skin. She whispered, *penga, hey*. She had to be more careful. She swore, in English, and then in Shona.

But there was one good thing. The sleep and the fear together had acted like electricity on her brain, and it was clear to her what she had to do now. It was like hunting in the bush: before anything else, you assessed the danger. Will clenched two filthy fists. So, before anything – before she ate, or slept again, or found somewhere to wash her hand, which was turning yellow round the puncture marks – she had to find the newspaper that woman had mentioned.

She walked on, looking warily around the street. There were plenty of newspapers strewn over the pavements and in the bus shelters, but they all turned out to be different. Londoners seemed to have an endless choice of sizes and colours for their newspapers. Some had colour pictures of women in lacy underwear; some had rows and rows of numbers and graphs. Neither looked right; it took her nearly two hours of searching and discarding and ducking into doorways before she found the right one. It was on the third page of a large greyish paper, *The Independent*. (Will felt gratified it was that one; it might be a good omen. Better *Independent* than the other that filled the bins, *Guardian*; guardian meant Miss Vincy, and Leewood, and rules she broke without knowing, and the endless list of women and girls who didn't want her.)

It was on the third page. *Monkey Escape at London Zoo: Link to Missing Schoolgirl.* The street she was now on was lined with houses; she crouched awkwardly against a stone wall and a plastic dustbin, and held the paper up to hide her face.

The article took up half the page. 'Two rare and valuable monkeys were found to have escaped through a hole cut in the enclosure roof.' An angry mother claimed her handbag had been stolen by one; the other had snatched a sandwich from a little girl, and both monkeys together had chased a boy through the reptile enclosure for half an hour before they were recaptured. Will grinned.

The director of the zoo was interviewed, and there was a picture of him, looking a little apoplectic, reassuring the public that all dangerous animals were secured by state-of-the-art electronic gating. There was a quote in bold print: 'We can confidently guarantee the safety of the public when the zoo reopens tomorrow: *very confidently indeed*.' Though Will thought he looked more sweaty than confident.

It was the second paragraph that was about her. A child's glove had been found inside the enclosure, and the nametape read 'Wilhelmina Silver'. Will swore under her breath, bit her lip. '*Oh, no, no, no. Oh sha, no!*' Wildcats didn't cry: no tear ducts.

Will sniffed wetly and turned back to the paper. She took care not to get drips on the newsprint. The article took a whole paragraph to describe her: 'Wilhelmina Silver went missing from the prestigious Leewood boarding school two days ago.' There was her passport photo; blurred and scowling, and a list of *notable features*: unusually large dark eyes; antipodean accent; heavily scarred knees. 'The school suggests that Wilhelmina can be easily recognised by her hair, which is severely tangled at the crown of the head and reaches past her knees.' At the bottom there was a number to call: 'anyone with any information is asked to come forward to the police.'

Will's heart started pounding with terror. It was that word again: *police*. The need to hide pressed down on Will's chest, and she looked unsteadily up and down the street. The houses loomed over her, all of them greyish-yellow and too tightly packed together (a lot like, Will thought, the Captain's false teeth, which he'd turned orange and black with nicotine. She bit her tongue. She didn't want to think about the farm.)

In front of each house was a large green plastic dustbin of the perfect size to hide in. She lifted the lid of one; dustbin stench belched out.

'*Sha!*'

Will backed away. She could still fit inside, on top of one of the bags. She tried to coax herself – soft-voiced like Lazarus to the horses – to climb on top of the black bags. Her legs didn't agree. They stayed where they were. Fine. If she couldn't hide, she'd have to make some kind of disguise. She could do nothing about the other things the article said she was: 'olive skinned', 'small and slight for her age' (which was what the Leewood girls meant when they said, *midget*), and 'likely to be noticeably dishevelled' (which meant, she guessed, unwashed). But there was one thing she could change, right now, something in her own power, and as Will thought of it, she felt hope rise in her chest. Her father would have said, *a nudge to the heart and a polish to the soul*; and the Captain would have spat, and nodded with closed eyes.

She dropped back down on her haunches against the bin, and sorted the Swiss army knife from the tangle in her pockets. Will gathered her hair in a bundle over her shoulder and hacked at it with the scissor part of the knife. They were blunt from cutting the wire at the zoo; just a few solitary wisps drifted onto the pavement. She prised out the knife instead with one bitten nail and sliced downwards at the hair over her eyes, tugging it taut with her swollen hand and hacking with the other. It worked. Chunks of brown fell on to the pavement. She looked the other way. It was despicable to cry about hair.

When she'd got it to shoulder length all round, Will stopped and ran her fingers through it. It felt strangely light, and smooth. She wished she had a mirror. It still felt too long to be much of a disguise: she probably didn't look very different.

Will took up the knife again in tight knuckles. It was harder cutting close to the head; but she gritted her teeth and kept hacking until she thought it was like the boy at the zoo's; three inches all round, except over her left ear where the knife had slipped and she was bald. She ran her fingers through it, tugged at it. Her neck felt oddly light. If she spat on her hands and used it as glue she could make it stand straight up, like the quills on a porcupine: or the hackles on a cat. Will grinned. She thought, *wildcat hair*. The grass on the farm used to be longer than this.

Lights were starting to flicker on in some of the houses now. She sank back against the wheelie bin. She thought, what next? *Think, Will.* But for the moment she could only feel: feel mostly how strong the wind was growing, and how it seemed to be blowing through her skin and lining her bones with frost.

She could see halfway down the street a red box, like one of the toilet cubicles at school, but with windows and a door that reached all the way to the floor. One of the windows was broken, but it might still be warmer than the pavement. Will bundled handfuls of her hair into her pockets and limped towards it.

Inside the box there was a smell of dying rodents, and urine, and – Will was amazed – a telephone. The telephone gave her an idea, though, and she searched through her pockets for the coins the tourists had given her. If she could work out how to call the number from the article, and if she disguised her voice then she could say she had spotted herself, somewhere else. Throw them off the scent, she thought. Sweep away her tracks, like if you were hunting impala with a gun by the waterhole.

Where could she have seen herself, though? She didn't know the names of any English towns, and she'd never thought to ask her father. There was so much she hadn't thought to ask, she thought angrily – about whether money was really important, and about how not to care about being hated, and how to live in the aching cold. Will spat, and coughed, then shook the thought away. Her father used to sing about it being a long way to Tipperary. But she didn't know if that was a place. It might, she thought, be a verb.

Will found a handful of cold coppers, but it didn't look enough. They had given her more than that, she knew, and she dug through her pockets. She started to unpack her shorts properly; knife, bits of straw, a sheaf of paper – Will stared at the paper. In one corner it said, *Daniel James*. Underneath that, in between doodles of lions and superheroes, was scribbled *Exclusive Property of Daniel James. 117 Clement Avenue. London. England. The World. The Universe.* And underneath, in capitals, KEEP OFF ON PAIN OF DEATH (Very Painful Death).

Will whispered, '*Unanki*. Excellent.' And there came stark realisation; it was easier, in this world, not to be alone.

Will burst out of the red box – calling the number wasn't important now – and hopped and limped through the streets until she found a small shop with newspapers in the window. It was grubby and cluttered, like the shops in Mutare; not at all like the great stone buildings she'd passed that day, which were more like African hospitals. Nobody looked up as she went in. The fat man at the desk kept reading a paper.

She quickly found a yellow and red roly-poly cake, and a plastic bottle of Coke. At home Coke came in glass bottles; Will marvelled at the lightness of this one, and tossed it into the air. The man behind the cash desk called out, 'Oi! You! You better be going to buy that, yeah?' and she jumped, and turned the same colour as the Coke label, and ducked down the next aisle. There she was desperately tempted by the jar of crunchy peanut butter, but it was two dollars – *pounds*, she corrected herself, and whispered it out loud to make herself remember, '*pounds*, hey' – and she needed the money for a map. At the counter she added the cheapest bar of chocolate, and laid everything in a row.

'And I'd like a map,' she said. 'Please, ja?'

The man said, 'Ayterzed, yeah?'

Will blinked.

'You want an Ayterzed? Or one of the touristy ones?'

'I'm not a tourist. Just a paper map.'

'Right you are.'

'Also –'

'Yes?'

'Um . . . what street are we on?'

'What street?' He smiled. 'Sure you're not a tourist?'

Will tried to smile back. 'Ja. Sure.'

'This is Sunnyfield Road. Page forty-two on the map, if you want to know.'

Will nodded. Page forty-two. 'That's everything, thank you.'

'Nine eighty nine, then.'

Will looked at the coins in her hand. There wasn't enough for it all. She put back the cake, blushing hotly.

The man tapped his fingers impatiently. 'You need a bag, son?'

'What? I mean, *yes*.' Son. She'd forgotten about the hair. Will tried to deepen her voice, to sound like a boy. 'Yes. A large one, please.'

'You what?'

'Yes, please.' It came out halfway between a growl and a burp. She tried again. '*Yes.*' It was like an engine revving.

The man looked at her suspiciously and laid the change on the counter, ignoring her outstretched hand.

'You all right, lad?' He glanced towards the open paper on his chair, and back at Will. 'Nothing on your mind?'

Will flushed again and shook her head. *Hush, chook* she thought; silence, now, was her best defence. Silence, and speed: she ran with her bag down the steps and into the street.

It was dark outside, and lamplights were starting to prick the sky: like overweight fireflies, thought Will. She'd never seen so many houses crushed so close together. She'd never seen a map of a city, either, but she was quick and had a hawk's sense of direction – 'my fierce little falcon,' her father used to say – and it wasn't difficult to work out a route. Will turned west and set off at a steady limp, holding the comic book in one tightly clenched fist.

CHAPTER TWENTY-FOUR

The house, when she found it, was exactly like every other house she'd passed. There was a narrow road separating it from another row of houses: and those looked exactly like every other house she had passed, too. Two hours of walking had given Will a very low opinion of English architecture.

It took her some time to find the right house. The numbering didn't go as she would have done it, one-two-three up one side and back down the other like a scale; instead it was odd on one side and even on the other, some with As and Bs tacked on at unexplained intervals. It was an ugly sort of way of labelling, Will thought; it was like the school: ordered insanity. She caught sight of her own scowl in a car window and shivered. The cold was eating her heart.

She pressed one finger against the doorbell of number 117.

Nothing happened.

She pushed again, with all five fingers; and again; and

knocked with both fists. A man and a woman walking arm in arm along the pavement stopped, murmured to each other, stared at her. Or was she just imagining it? Will tried to hide her face; but it was impossible, now, with no hood and no hair. Increasingly desperate, Will tried the door. It was locked. Of course. England was a land of locks. She was just about to ring the bell for a seventh time when the door opened and Daniel stood on the doorstep.

'Yes?'

'I –' To her fury she began to stutter and blush, 'I. I was wondering, ja –'

He shielded his hand from the yellow glare of the hallway light. 'Bloody hell. It's you!'

He knew some impressive swear words, Will thought. He ran through them in a voice of awed surprise. 'You! What do you want? Didn't you see that thing in the paper? I *knew* it was you! Lizzie didn't believe me. I knew it! There's police searching everywhere, you know.'

'I know. I want –' Will clenched both fists so tightly that her nails bit through the paper of the comic and broke the skin on her palms. 'I need help.'

'What sort of help?' He didn't seem to guess how much it took to say it.

'Your help. I need somewhere to sleep, ja, and somewhere to think.'

'Oh.' He glanced backwards into the hall. 'Right. The thing is, though . . .'

'*Please.*'

'It's just, my Nan would slaughter me. And my sister Lizzie's upstairs. She's got about three thousand friends up there. They'd call the police if they saw you.'

'Why? Why would they do that?'

'I dunno. There's a station down the road and they fancy one of the sergeants.' And then, 'What happened to your hair? Where's it gone?'

'In my pocket. With some chocolate I bought for you.' She felt for it. 'They might be a bit mixed up.' Will decided not to tell him about the police, the running, the exhaustion. 'It's easier to be invisible, ja, if you're a boy.'

Daniel nodded. He seemed to take it as a compliment to his sex. She said, 'I made it like yours. A' – what was it called? – 'a tribute. You were a major influence on my work.'

'Yeah? Really?' and he laughed, harder than she expected, spraying the doorstep with spit. He said, 'Look. Have you been followed?' She shook her head. 'Then I guess you'd better get inside. Nan's gone to the chip shop. We'll be safe for five minutes. She walks slow.'

Will followed him, past a bicycle and a backpack, past a pile of school shirts and a football, through a narrow door into a kitchen.

'Do you need food?' said Daniel. 'Will? What sort of thing do you eat?' There was no answer. 'Will?'

'What?' Will was entranced by the kitchen. 'What? Oh, anything, ja.' She tore herself away from something that looked like an interesting torture instrument with fake-gold fake-handwriting up one side. *Supa-Wizz Electric Blender*. 'Do you have biltong? Simon and me used to eat that when we were tired. It's just meat and salt.'

'No. We've got sausages in a tin.'

'Can I put them in your *Supa-Wizz Electric Blender*?'

'No.'

'Why not? What would happen?'

'My gran would notice. You don't cross my gran. She's fierce.'

'Oh,' she said. And then, 'Those chairs . . . they look comfortable, ja?'

'I guess, yeah.'

'Could you sleep in them?'

He laughed. 'Subtle.'

'What?'

'*You* couldn't. I'm sorry, yeah, honestly, but my gran would *definitely* notice. You don't really blend in to the furniture.'

'Oh. Who sleeps in the stable?'

'What stable?'

'The one attached to your house, ja?'

'That's the garage. The car's in it. Nobody drives it, not since my granddad died last month.'

'Then I'll sleep there,' said Will. Daniel raised his eyebrows: she had tried to sound authoritative and persuasive at once and her voice had come out like Mrs Robinson's. She added, softer, 'Please, hey, Daniel?'

'You can't. There's no light.'

'I *can*. Please. I've got a torch: see, there. Please. You have to let me. It's important. This isn't a game.'

'I can't just –' Dan paused. Upstairs he had a set of plastic Indians. There was one with a knife in his hand, crouched to spring. This girl looked like that: she looked ready to fight.

'All right.' He started digging in a drawer for candles and matches; they wouldn't do much, but might give a bit of warmth. 'But I can't get you any blankets. My gran'd notice they were gone. You'd have to sleep under your coat.'

'Fine. That's fine. Quick, ja.'

'Where is it, anyway? Your coat?'

Will could feel her ears turning red. 'I'll be fine. I just need to be inside, and to sleep, and to think. I can't plan in the rain. It's like ice.'

'You don't have a coat?' She was thinner than anyone he'd ever seen, and her lips were lined with purple. She'd freeze to death. 'How can you not have a coat?'

Will kept herself from throwing the *Supa-Wizz*

Electric Blender at his head; but she found it was surprisingly difficult not to. 'It's fine! Can you just show me the way, ja? Please. And quick, hey. Before your grandmother gets back.'

He said, 'Don't rush me. I hate being rushed. Wait – you can have my granddad's coat, if you like. It's that one; on the hook. No, not that one; that's my sister's,' and Will dropped the beautiful fluff-hooded jacket as though it were a dead snake. He stared at her. 'What's wrong with you?'

'I don't like girls' things. I don't like girls.'

'That's ridiculous.' He picked up the blue coat, and unhooked another one. 'You're a girl yourself, aren't you? My gran says only cowards hate themselves.' When Will said nothing, only stared with those unblinking brown eyes, he turned away, saying, 'Here – this one's my granddad's.'

It was enormous, and smelt of cigarettes and dust. Will wrapped herself in it; it went round her twice. Despite the urgency in her chest, she grinned. It was like wearing courage.

He was watching her, and as they crossed the square of rubble that was the back garden he said, 'Weren't you cold, before?'

'Ja. Freezing. Especially at nights.'

'Scared?'

'No.'

He looked sceptical. 'Yeah, right.'

'Yes. Of being caught, ja. Not of anything else.'

He led her into a square of grass behind the house and round to the garage door. 'The hinges creak.' Dan pulled the door back and forth. 'Hear that? That can give you warning. If it's me, I'll knock twice first. If you hear the creak without a knock, it's someone else, and you'll have to escape round the back garden. Can you get out of the window?'

Will didn't think that was worth answering. Windows were her speciality. She said, 'Thanks. And I'll need water. I've done something to my ankle, I think; and the blisters are septic.' They had gone from plump transparent cushions to deflated brown patches with loose skin. She was more worried about them than she wanted to admit. 'And I cut my hand. There's pus.'

'Pus?'

'Ja. Don't you have pus in England? It's like . . . I dunno . . . yellow blood. It means there's an infection.'

'Right. OK.' He sounded flustered in the dark. He sounded young. 'Look, I've got to go. Gran'll be back in a second, and it's my day to lay the table. If I don't do it, she'll notice something's going on. She's fierce, my gran.'

'Ja. You said.' Will thought she liked the sound of her.

'Did I? Well, she *is*. But I'll bring water, and some food, in about an hour, yeah?'

At the door he stopped. 'One thing. If you're a boy now, what am I supposed to call you now?'

Will looked out from under the musty weight of the corduroy coat. Her chest was thawing now. For the first time in what felt like months, Will laughed properly. 'You call me Will,' she said.

Alone in the garage, Will dozed, woke, dozed, explored. The silence was complete, and once she had breathed hot air down into her coat, it was not unbearably cold. There was a box of spanners, and some bicycle lights that didn't appear to work, and a box full of damp comics.

She fished some out, and trained the light of the torch on one. She was astonished to find that she was too happy to read. Without warning, Will found that the feeling of being watched and disliked had left her; and along with it, the feeling of being always wrong, and the loneliness that had filled her chest with black tar. Will thought, why should it hurt so much to be hated? She had a feeling it was an important question, but before she could begin to think of an answer the garage door crashed open.

Will was up and across the floor and crouched behind the car before the door was halfway up – but even so – 'I can see your feet, you know,' said Daniel.

'Ja, well.' Will stood up. 'It's your fault. You forgot to knock,' but he could hear from the shapes of her words that she was grinning. 'There's nowhere to hide, anyway. I wouldn't have fit in the toolbox.'

'I'll bring a big cardboard box, later. I got you food.' He sounded much less bewildered than before. His voice was thick with excitement as he dropped to his haunches beside her.

'What's this?' said Will.

'Beans on toast. Do you eat beans?'

Will sniffed it. It smelt all right – wonderful, in fact, sweet and salty at the same time – but she hesitated. She wished it had been an apple, or plain bread. This would be difficult to eat neatly. It was important, she felt, that she eat the Leewood way, because it was important – quiveringly important – that Daniel like her. She wished she'd brought some paper napkins.

She groped round in the dark. 'What are you doing? What is it?' said Daniel.

'I was just looking – they must be here – for the knife and fork.'

'I didn't bring any.' He sounded angry. 'I couldn't take them without someone noticing, could I? It's not like we've got mountains of silver, you know.'

'Oh!' she'd said the wrong thing. 'No, ja. Just. Ja. I don't want to make a mess.'

'I wouldn't have thought you were one of *those* girls. Lizzie's like that; she always wants to be the perfect one.'

'No!' Will put her plate down with a thump. If he was Simon she would've had him by the hair by now. 'They said. At the school, ja. *Manners are a form of thanks*.'

'Are you being funny? That's just for adults. I don't care if you get sauce all over your face. You can get it in your bloody *ears* if you want to.'

'Oh. Nobody *said* that, ja. Nobody told me.'

'Well, now I've told you.' She could hear him smiling in the dark. She felt herself strengthened by it. 'Eat,' he said.

The beans were too hot, but Will was painfully hungry. She could feel the skin on the roof of her mouth burning off in little shreds, but they were so filling, and so sweet and deliciously solid . . . She looked up at Daniel laughing.

'What?'

'You've got sauce on your eyebrows.'

Will threw a bean at him. Even in the dim light she was accurate; she'd been deadly with an air rifle back home. 'And now so do you,' she said.

CHAPTER TWENTY-FIVE

Will did not hear the car that drew up just before midnight.

Daniel did: he couldn't sleep, or think about anything except the filthy girl alone in the garage. He should have given her his duvet, he thought. Or his curtains, to use as a tent; he could have unhooked them easily. The wind was battering at the house, and she might die of cold. He was just swinging himself out of bed when the noise of the bell cut through the house and he reached the landing in time to see his grandmother at the spy hole.

'*Daniel!* Daniel, get your young self down here!'

He joined her at the spy hole. Two policemen's helmets hovered at eye level.

His heart dropped to the floor. His knees followed it. 'Daniel!' His grandmother hauled him up again. 'This is not the time to be sitting down for a tea break.' His grandmother whispered, harsh with fear, 'What've you done? If you've been out with those hoodlums again I warn you, lad; I'll stop your pocket money until you're old enough to draw a pension.'

'I've not! Not for months, gran. I *told* you I hadn't.'

'If you have, lad . . .' She glared at him as she tugged at the door.

But it wasn't that at all: the stockier of the two men held out a blurred photograph. 'We have been notified, madam, that the missing schoolgirl – you will've read about it – may be concealed in your garage.'

'What?' said Daniel's grandmother.

'The missing schoolgirl – Wilhelmina Silver.'

'And you are saying what?' Mrs James was fierce to make up for the fright. She moved to shield Daniel from them. 'Are you calling me a kidnapper?'

'No, madam. But a man and a woman saw a person partially answering her description outside your house earlier this evening. It seems they debated for some time about calling us.'

'And why would that be? '

The policemen looked uncomfortable. 'It seems the girl had become bald since running away.' The old woman snorted. He continued, 'Nonetheless, they're sure it was her face. They say the eyes were unmistakable.'

'There is no runaway schoolgirl in this house, officer: be she bald, bearded or moustached.'

'Ah, yes; but her school says the girl is like a wild

animal. She might easily have broken in through a window.'

'And be living in the garage? And eating what, tell? The pliers? Or the Christmas decorations?'

'Please keep your temper, madam. If you could just give us the key.'

'I'm giving you nothing.'

The policemen exchanged looks. 'Right. Then if you could come and unlock it for us, madam?'

'We do have a search warrant.' That was the wiry, aggressive one.

Mrs James transferred her glare to the second police-man.

'I suppose I could do that, yes. Stay here, Daniel.'

'What? No! I'm coming with you.'

'Daniel! Stay here, I said.' But she didn't sound too furious. Daniel thought he could risk it, and followed three steps behind into the night.

His grandmother flung the garage door wide open. The policemen pushed forward, grunting. And Daniel braced himself to run.

'There you see. Nobody there.'

Daniel opened his eyes. It was true. And there was nowhere she could be hiding; no matter how small, an African runaway will not fit into a biscuit-tin already full of screwdrivers. The men waved their torches around in a resentful sort of way.

'Look under the car,' said the sharp-faced one, though they could all see there was nothing except an oil leak. Daniel felt his courage rise. He was on the point of delighted laughter when the wiry officer said, 'And if you could unlock the boot, please, madam?'

The old woman looked scathingly at them. 'No, I could not. The catch is broken. It needs a kick,' and as one of the policemen stepped forwards, '*No*, thank you. Daniel'll do it.'

Daniel whispered, 'Oh, no. No, *no*,' because he knew with sudden certainty where Will must be. His mouth tasted of vomit. He tapped at the bumper with his toe. 'I can't. It's stuck.'

'Oh, come on, kid. Give it a bit of muscle.'

He thumped, hard, at the wrong part of the boot. 'It's broken. See? How could Will have got in if it's glued shut?'

'Will? Who's Will?'

The wiry policeman swung his torch into Daniel's face. 'What did you just say?'

Daniel's face stretched with horror. 'I –' His grandmother's left eye gave him a warning look. 'I thought – you said – isn't that what you said the girl's name was?' he said.

'I see.'

'Right.'

'Step aside, please.' They advanced.

'Move aside, kid. We're going to need to take a look in that boot.'

Daniel saw he had no choice. He clenched his eyes shut and gave it a proper thump. With a shriek of rust, it opened.

'Oh,' said the first policeman. And the second policeman added, '*Ah.*' They looked down at two plastic bags and a patch of spilt soap powder.

'*Quite.*' His grandmother snorted. 'Will that be all, gentlemen? Or do you not think you've disturbed us enough for one night? Would you like us to prise open the gutters? Dig up the floor? Sing the national anthem?' His grandmother had a kind of ferocious beauty, despite being less than five foot, and as she herded them out before her he heard her saying, 'and you, lad – your boots need polishing. What, will you tell me, do we pay taxes for?'

Daniel followed them out of the garage door and slammed it shut behind him. He waited; there were the sounds of increasingly panicked apology; the low rumble of his grandmother's fiercest voice; and the front door slamming. A car started. Dan reopened the garage door and peered into the darkness. Without the policemen's torches the garage was black and icy.

'Will?' He didn't dare shout. He hissed, '*Will?* Are you here?'

'Daniel? *Daniel?*' Her voice sounded less musical

than before, he thought; flat and shaken. 'I'm caught.'

The voice came from outside the open window. There was a scrabbling, like birds on a roof, and Will's face appeared, upside-down and pale in the moonlight. 'Daniel! Oh, thank goodness, hey. I think I'm on a sort of gutter. Help, please! It keeps creaking; I'm too heavy.'

'What were you *doing*, Will?'

'I tried to get right up on to the roof but my bootlace got caught. I don't know what to do.' Will's soft eyes looked desperately into Dan's face. 'Can you cut it?'

He stood on a chair. She was lying along the gutter, covered in leaf mould and surrounded by roosting pigeons (he stared: why hadn't they flown off? Or made frightened pigeon noises, and warned the police?). It was a long drop to the concrete below. 'Hold on,' he said, 'I'll get the kitchen scissors. Hold on, OK?'

'I can't. No! Don't go. There's a penknife in my pocket,' said Will, 'hold my shoulders – ja – I can reach it.' She had to shift her weight to get at her pocket and the gutter shuddered and groaned. The pigeons stared reproachfully.

Will held her breath. 'I – wait – *penga* . . .' The gutter settled, but a few inches lower than before. Two puffs of relief misted the night air. Will gripped the knife in her teeth and spoke round it. 'Can you reach round and cut me free?'

It took five endless minutes of cutting and waiting and listening before Will was disentangled. She still clung to the roof, 'Wait! I'm at a funny angle.' Her voice was tight and breathless. 'I don't know if I can slide back in.' Her voice sounded as though she was fighting tears. 'I think something snapped in my ankle. Not a bone –'

'A ligament, maybe?' Dan was good at science.

Will glared. 'Help, please, ja?'

'No need to get angry. You're safe now. Hold on. You OK? I'll hold on to your wrist.' Daniel piled the biscuit tins on his chair and reached further out. 'Give me your wrist. Yeah. Good. Slowly. Now your elbow.' He tugged at her sleeves and Will slid towards the casement. She kicked at the gutter with one foot. He caught her by the back of her coat and lowered her the rest of the way.

So Daniel was like she was, Will thought: stronger than he looked.

They sat together on the concrete floor.

'What time is it now?'

Will peered at the sky. 'After midnight. Before two.'

'I should go to bed, or Gran'll notice. Are you warm enough?'

'Ja, thanks.' Will looked at him in the pitch black. She said, 'Thank you, ja.' The second thank you, he thought, meant something else.

'No problem. You should go to sleep. I'll try to bring you tea and something to eat in the morning. I sing in a choir, but I should be able to get out of it.' He turned back at the door. 'You do drink tea, yeah?' The girl seemed more like a cat than a person: she was like a whisper, or a starjump. 'Would you rather have milk? I could find a saucer: or do you know about mugs?'

'Ja! Of course. Tea is good. At home we had red bush tea; rooibos, you know?' He didn't, but said he'd look in the kitchen cupboards. He added, 'Sleep well. Don't run off in the night, yeah? You will still be here?'

'What? Of course, ja! Don't let the mosquitoes bite. Sleep tight, hey.'

But Will had lied. She was getting good at it. She and Simon had never lied, at home. They'd despised Peter, who lied about pointless things, and was bad at it. But it seemed it was only easy to be honest when you were happy.

She hauled herself to her feet – foot, in fact, and even the uninjured one felt rough and raw, as though she'd walked through the padding and into the bone – and hopped to the window. The windowsill was rough unpainted wood and she bit her tongue not to wince at the splinters. She pulled herself halfway up but her arms gave way and she dropped down again. She tried again. Failed again. She couldn't do it; without the mad-adrenalin rush of panic, she was stuck here.

She sank down in a corner, and gripped her stubbled hair, and forced her thoughts to steady themselves into columns. She needed real, solid plans. No more cartwheeling round London. This wasn't a game. *Think, Will,* she told herself, and then, when she could only shiver, *courage, chook.* In the *Bad* column: the police were clever. They would come back. She was sure. This wasn't a book; they didn't just give up and go home. And she was just a child, and alone. In the *Good* column: Dan was funny and kind, and obviously not stupid. But – *Bad*: he was unlikely to be able to provide things like aeroplanes. And he looked the sort of boy who got flustered in a fight. And – *Bad*: it would now be impossible, she saw, to get on an aeroplane home even when she did have the money; they did checks at airports, and – *Bad* column – they'd be on the lookout. Unless – her face brightened and shone in the blackness – she could get a fake passport. But where did a bald schoolgirl go to commit fraud? It was impossible. The world was *bad*.

What else was there? With a swollen ankle, and a septic hand and the beginnings of a black eye and bald patches, she didn't think she'd make a prime candidate for adoption. What else? She wrestled with the thought until she could barely breathe. It was like slamming her chest against a brick wall, and she could see no way over it. Will fell asleep, in the end, backed into a concrete corner, with the wind crashing against the window, and her last waking thought was of her own room back home, and the dance of the dust, and the window without glass. She would not have been surprised if her head had swollen with longing and burst in her sleep.

CHAPTER TWENTY-SIX

Will opened her eyes to find the world was still dark, and her heart was still intact. But no night was this black. She closed her eyes again; and opened them again to nothingness, and breathed in a mouthful of something heavy and gagging. She thrashed, and spat. There was a clunk, and a crack of breaking china, and quiet laughter. Panicking, Will tore her head free from the coat and saw that she was lying in bright morning light. There was a broken mug at her side and a plate of toast with something brown spread thickly on it. But Will saw neither of these, because sitting in a pool of spilt tea, there was a woman. She was wrinkled all over, hands and face and clothes; just like a slept-in bed, Will thought. She was smiling.

The woman said, 'Hello, Will.'

Will leapt to her feet. The coat tangled round her legs, and she stumbled over her own knees, choking. 'Ah, *sha*!', and thudded down on to the concrete floor.

The woman hadn't moved. 'That sounded painful, Will.'

'No! My name's not Will,' Will gasped from the floor. 'I'm a friend of Daniel's. My name's . . .' What was a boy's name? She could think of none. 'Wilbur.' *Wilbur?*

'No, it's not, my dear. Your name is Wilhelmina Silver.' For so minuscule an old woman, her voice was firm. It was a voice to stake a life on, rough and lilting and deep. Will didn't know what you called a voice like that; the old woman would have said it was Irish, with a shadow of South London, and a chunk of Scots.

'Please.' There was no air in Will's lungs. She whispered, 'Are you going to call the police? Please don't call them, ja?' She swatted at the tears that had appeared on her face. 'Please.'

'Come on, dear one. Sit up, now, and calm down. Eat your toast. Wrap yourself in this.'

Will stared out from underneath the coat. The woman's hair was thin and wispy, and she was almost bald in places, but her eyelashes were thicker than Simon's, and the eyes were the green of gin bottles and banana leaves. She could see why Daniel – sharp-faced and tall as he was – was so in awe of this woman.

'Eat, Will. Food makes the world look brighter. You must be hungry.'

Now that she thought about it, Will realised how

hungry she had been – for weeks: a dozen different kinds of hungry. She ate the toast in three bites, without chewing. The woman smiled steadily.

'What's this one?' Will waved a second piece. 'In here?'

'Hazelnut spread.'

It tasted hopeful: thick, nutty hope.

'Do you want another?'

'Ja! Yes. Yes, please.'

'We'll go in in a second. Finish up that last piece. No hurry, though.'

Will thought the woman's voice sounded like the opposite of hurry. It was thick and soft: like the hazelnut spread.

'I'm sure you can manage some jam, too, and there's a boiled egg in the kitchen, my love, with your name on it.'

'Thank you.' Will said. 'It was a long walk.' Her bones felt hollow.

'Yes! And how did you know the way?'

'It was easy. I bought an ayterzed.'

'Ah, child! At your age I couldn't have found my own front door with a compass.' Will grinned into her chin. She tried not to look smug.

The woman said, 'Come on, then. Start at the beginning. I want to hear your story. A story's a good return for a breakfast.'

That seemed fair. Will wrapped her arms round her chest, and felt the warm skin of her own spine, and told the woman everything, slowly at first, and then with her words bumping into each other in her hurry: about Cynthia Vincy (who was to blame for her father's death) and the school (where girls sat two by two in rows of spite, and where everything was rigid and flimsy, 'both, ja, at once, like cardboard dolls') and to here, now, in the refuge of the garage.

'And now, ja, I'm caught,' Will said, and she could not stop her chest shaking a little. 'I can't get home, because I haven't got money, so I can't bribe people for a new passport. And I don't know . . . I don't know how it works. Aeroplanes, and money, and everything.' She scowled at the floor to thwart possible tears. 'And I won't go back to school.'

The woman stood up. It took some time, but Will didn't want to offer to help. It would have been presumptuous, maybe.

'Come into the house, dear heart, and we'll get you a new mug of tea. No, leave the pieces. Daniel will see to them when he comes home.'

'Daniel!' She'd forgotten. 'Where is Daniel?'

'He sings in the church choir. There's a wedding, and I said he was to let you sleep. I promised he'd see you soon. He fought like a wildcat, but I told him I would look after you.'

'Did he tell you I was here?' Will was suddenly angry. 'He *swore* not to.'

'He did not. But I'm quicker in the brain than I look. This creaking old body is deceptive.'

'Oh. How *did* you know?'

'I can tell when my boy's lying. It's a talent the old acquire. One of the few compensations for being rickety.' The old woman led Will through the scrubby back garden and into the kitchen. 'This way; up on that stool. You sit yourself comfortably. Now, let's have a look at that ankle.'

Will stared blankly. 'How did you know –' She hadn't told the woman about her foot.

'I told you, love; I know how important it is to notice things. You know that, too, I would guess. It takes one to know one. Boots off, girl.'

When Will was wedged in a chair with one foot in a bucket of warm water, the woman said, 'Keep eating, child. Do you want jam on the next? Good.' With her back to Will and her hands busy with the bread knife, she added, 'Can I give you a piece of advice, Will?'

Will looked at the floor.

'No? No, chickadee? I can't give you advice?'

'I – I don't want to be rude, ja. Please don't think it's rude –' The warmth in Will's skin was coming back.

'But? There's a but coming, is there not?'

'It's just . . . I don't think you can say anything I

haven't thought of, ja. You'll tell me to go back to the school.'

'Ah.'

'But you can't understand –' Will reached up to pull at her hair but there was only air and so she scrubbed instead at her face with sharp brown knuckles, 'you can't understand, what the sun was like.' She didn't know if she could explain: what it was like when crickets sang every day, and you couldn't feel where you stopped and the sunshine began.

'I don't . . . I can't describe it – imagine if there's just trees, ja and grass and boys and bats, ja, and warthogs, and dragonflies. And nobody hates you. And you could run, ja, or ride, for miles, and if you got lost, the women just gave you mangoes and aspirin and directions – and once, I fell out of a tree, and they gave me a Ridgeback, to *keep*, ja – you can't *know*.' Will discovered her face was turning red with the rubbing, and sat on her hands. 'It was like living in pure blue.'

The woman said nothing, just stared and smiled and nodded.

Will's body felt suddenly limp and helpless. 'I won't go back to school. Those girls . . . they weren't real, ja . . . it was like they were afraid they'd break themselves. They weren't like the boys in the farm.'

'But, sweet Will – is strawberry jam all right, child? Good. No, sit down. I'll make it – I was going to say, my dear one: are you sure? Because, you know, people are more different than we give them credit for. Kindness comes in so many different disguises.' The old woman smiled. 'If you can find your way here with a sprained ankle and an *A to Z*, surely you can find some goodness in those girls?'

'No! You don't understand. That's not how school works.'

'Don't I? Are you sure?'

'Yes! And I'm not pretty like they are – I'd just make them feel prettier, and I'd get uglier, and I'd stop believing, ja, that life was beautiful.'

'Oh, my dear –'

'Ja. So,' Will interrupted. 'So I can't take advice. If I can't stay here, I'll run again.' She kicked at the water in the bowl and tried to smile. 'But – ma'am – I don't want to be rude.'

The old woman smiled and said, 'Don't worry about that. You be as rude as you like.'

Will stared at the jam pot. She wouldn't look the old woman in the face. She didn't know what would happen if she did.

'You're right, Will. I was going to say you have to go back. Much as I would love to keep you for my own. I was going to say, I and my Daniel could visit you, at the weekends. You could adopt us, if you so wanted. But you do have to go back. In fact you don't have a choice. This is a land of compulsory education, my love. Do you know what that means?'

'Ja. But – ach. It's a land of compulsory everything.'

'What?'

'Rules . . .' Will could barely talk through her mouthful of sadness. 'You only have rules.'

The old woman lifted Will's foot out of the bowl and set it on her lap. 'You must say if this hurts; it's an antiseptic. It should only sting a little. Listen, sweet Will. Here's the advice I was going to give. Go back to your school – I know, it hurts,' because Will had given a dry hard sob that had nothing to do with the disinfectant. 'Can I tell you why I have to send you back?'

Will set her jaw. 'You just said. Laws.'

'No, dear heart. Laws can always be got round. It is because, Will, I think you're too brave to be a runaway.'

That wasn't what Will had expected. She said, 'I – what?'

'It is real life that takes the real courage, little wildcat. School is very difficult. But that's because it takes toughness and patience. It's what life is, my love. Although life is very beautiful, it is also very difficult.'

Will blinked, surprised. 'That's what Captain Browne used to say. He used to say, ja: *life isn't all mangoes and milktarts.*'

'Then he was a clever man, though it sounds like he had terrible taste in wives.'

Will felt the corners of her mouth twitch.

'If you keep running like this, you'll exhaust your own heart. I promise you – I swear it on the lives of my grandchildren – that life is best when you're not trying to hide. Hiding and panic go together. There is nothing in this world that is worse than panic.'

That Will knew was true. She stopped staring at the jam pot.

'I do know how difficult school can be, my love. I hated it myself. If you go back, it won't be like cartwheeling in sunshine. It would be more like cartwheeling into the wind.'

'Into a hurricane,' said Will. 'Into a *tempest*.'

'Yes, sometimes. But it would be the best possible training. It would make your arms strong.'

Will said, 'Oh. Ja. I see.'

'And your heart. You could build a cartwheeling wildcat heart.'

'Ja.' Will swallowed.

'Wouldn't that be worth fighting for? Wouldn't that be worth going back for?'

'I don't know. I think so.' Will felt her heart straining against her ribs. 'Yes. Ja. I do.'

'I think so too. Pass me the Dettol – beside you – no, that's maple syrup – thank you. May I have a look at that hand? We need to get you in shape for cartwheeling.'

CHAPTER TWENTY-SEVEN

Will's desk at the front of the classroom had been like a bruise. Nobody dared touch it. Superstitious, a few girls left peace offerings; a pen that wrote in four different colours, a new pencil case, a handful of notes. 'She's not *dead*,' said Samantha, 'we didn't *kill* her. You're being *ridiculous*': but she found herself looking at icy silence.

Louisa added a handful of chocolate coins. She didn't meet anyone's eye. Joanna said, 'It should be Sam, really, who leaves something. She started it.'

Samantha tinkled out her laugh.

Zoe said, 'For goodness' sake, laugh properly.'

'*What* did you say?'

'That's a false laugh. Like a false moustache,' Zoe said, and Hannah added, 'Only stupider. I'm going outside. Come on, Zoe.'

The twins went outside to practise cartwheels. After a while, the rest followed them.

***

The girls were watching from the radiators by the up-stairs window when the car drew up. They saw a tiny, bald child climb out, holding in one hand what looked like the last bite of a jam sandwich. They saw it turn to the old woman at the steering wheel – a woman, they could see, whose nose barely reached above the steering-wheel – and kiss her many times.

'Who is that?' said Samantha. 'Are they letting boys into Leewood?'

The child shook out its legs – dressed in boy's jeans several sizes too large – swallowed the bite of the sand-wich, scrubbed at its eyes with the knuckles of its ban-daged hand, waved with the unbandaged one, turned away – grinned, shouted something, waved again – and started to limp towards the headmistress's office.

Just as the figure reached the main door the girls upstairs saw it burst open, and Miss Blake fly out. The child's body was swept off its feet and swung in a circle, so that its legs fanned out like the brim of a hat. Sobs of laughter flew up to the window. Then the child was set down and kissed, hard, on the forehead; shaken, hard, by the elbows: swept up again, and carried bodily inside.

Samantha dragged her lips back from where they had hung, limp with shock, near her chin. 'Was that the *savage*?'

'Can't be.'

'It was,' said Zoe.

'Can't be. It had no hair.'

'It was,' said Hannah.

'Can't be. They said she wasn't coming back.'

'It was.'

At second break, Samantha came looking for Will. Will was crouched under the form tutor's desk. A letter had come from Simon the day before: Will had to be alone to read it properly. Her hands fumbled with the joy of it as she unfolded the earth-stained paper.

Samantha's voice said, 'Will? Are you in here?'

Part of Will was tempted to stay still and say nothing. Nobody was as good as she was at staying still. But she hadn't come back to hide, she told herself. 'Ja. Just a second.' Will cracked her head against the desk. 'Ow. *Sha.*' She pushed the letter into the waistband of her skirt for later. As she crawled out, injured foot first, Will tried to summon up every inch of courage she had, up into her chest.

Samantha was standing in the doorway, stony-faced and awkward. 'I've been told to say I'm sorry.'

Will wasn't sure what she had been expecting. 'Oh. Ja.' Part of her – the same part that would have liked to have stayed under the desk – would have liked to have held on to her resentment. Part of her would have liked to have spat. But carrying resentment, Will told herself, would be like carrying a pocket full of broken glass. It was a good image, and she grinned; and thought, *you can't cartwheel in broken glass*.

To her astonishment, Samantha smiled back. 'Not just about the bath. I'm sorry about everything.'

'What?'

'Your dad, and all that. We didn't know.'

Will said, 'Ja. Oh. Ja.' Forgiving people, it turned out, was easier than it looked. But then so was breaking into a zoo. Things were easier once you tried them, Will thought.

Mrs Robinson hunted the headmistress down in her office. She stood in front of Miss Blake, her nostrils clenched shut with determination. She had come to see that justice was done. 'What are you going to do about Wilhelmina, Angela?'

'Do?'

'With any other runaway child, Angela, we would be seriously considering expulsion. I understand her circumstances are unusual, but –'

'Exactly, Roz. She is unusual.'

'Not so very extraordinary, Angela.'

'Have you ever seen her smile?

Mrs Robinson didn't answer directly. 'She seems a sullen child.'

'Does she?'

'She is astonishingly ignorant for her age. She seems spectacularly underdeveloped mentally. I have been wondering if she would not do better in a special school.'

'I see. Yes, Roz, she is young for her age. In some ways. In other ways, I'd say she's very old. Could you have survived on your own? In the African bush? Or sleeping rough in London? That's the stuff of warriors, surely?'

Mrs Robinson didn't answer directly. 'I've been wondering if we should look into psychotherapy.'

'Mm . . .'

'Mm? What's that supposed to mean, Angela? A yes or a no?'

'You haven't seen her smile, have you?'

'What's your point, Angela?'

'Her smile. It could burn holes through ice.' Miss Blake ran a hand through her hair, thinking. The girl's smile was like a love letter to the world. 'Will's not sullen, Roz.'

'I beg to differ. She is stubborn, and silent to the point of rudeness. I find her extremely difficult to like.'

'It is possible that the feeling is mutual. Personally, I find her beautiful.'

'*Beautiful?*'

'Beautiful, yes.'

'The child was never going to win Little Miss Greater London, Angela, but now! That *hair*.'

'Mm.'

'*What* is that noise supposed to mean?'

'I was thinking, Roz, how astonishingly blind humans can be. I recommend you book an appointment with your optician.' Mrs Robinson's spectacles were made of clear glass: she wore them to give herself an air of authority. It was perhaps because of this, Miss Blake realised later, that her deputy's reply was hissed with such venomous politeness.

'I must remind you, *Angela*, that you do not own this school. A headmistress is not a proprietor. I have been here more than twice your time, and if you are suggesting I have been negligent at any point in my care of Wilhelmina, I would ask you to make a complaint in writing to the board of governors. *Immediately*! I will not,' and her voice became shrill, 'I will *not* bear with innuendo and calumny.'

'Oh for Christ's sake, Roslyn! It wasn't personal. I was just saying – hold the front page and send out a news bulletin! – school is a lonely place to be.' Angela Blake sighed. 'I'm sorry. I didn't mean to sound juvenile. Will is not sullen. She is miserable. A common complaint, after all.'

'You make it sound like a disease.'

'Do I? My hope, Roz, is that the girl's soul will prove contagious.'

***

Will sat silent through the morning's lessons. She could feel that every eye was watching her. Possibly, she thought, they were expecting her to attack them. To prove she wouldn't, she sat as still as possible. They were like impala, she thought. She mustn't frighten them away.

When lunchtime came she slipped quietly into her old seat at the empty end of the lunch table. Five girls stared hard at their laps as she slid by.

Will smelt her soup. It was something tasteless and indeterminate. Potato, she thought – and dipped in a finger, stirred it, blew on it. She found her mouth wouldn't open enough for her to eat it.

There was a crash; two crashes. Will looked up just as the twins put down their trays, one on either side of her.

'Can we sit here?'

'Oh.' Will looked up at them. They had long, clever, complicated faces. '*Ja*. I mean. Yes. Of course.'

They sat, awkwardly, tripping over their chairs.

'So . . .' said one twin: and the other added, 'I,' just as Will said, 'Did you –' Together all three said, 'Oh, go ahead . . .'

'So you came back, then?' That was Zoe, Will thought: the one with slightly longer hair, and more bitten fingernails.

'Ja.'

'*Obviously* she did, Zoe.'

Will sunk lower into her chair, wondering whether they were waiting for her to speak. She felt her heart writhe, and wished she could think of something to say – anything at all – but all her words (English, Shona, just *noises*, even) – had left her.

The silence grew louder.

Then – 'Did you know there was an assembly about you?'

'No.' Will wasn't sure she knew what an assembly was.

'Yeah! They thought you might've been kidnapped. They called the police; and then Louisa said you might have run away –'

'And Miss Blake said, Why would you have done that? – and then –'

'You could hear her shouting from the North block –'

'From the North *Pole*. She went purple.'

'We thought maybe you'd gone back to Africa –'

'On a boat, or something –'

'Or hidden in those overhead lockers on a plane –'

'And Sam said, that's ridiculous – and we said, it wasn't, actually, because you were the sort of girl who might do anything –'

'*I* said that.'

'Ja,' said Will, 'I wanted to – I would've – but –'

'We're glad you didn't, Will.' And the other one said,

'That's all we wanted to say, really. That we're glad,' and then before Will could reply they added together, 'Really glad – *ja*.'

They must have planned it. 'Oh,' said Will. 'Oh. *Ndatenda hangu*. I mean – ja. *Tatenda*, ja? Thank you. I – ja. Thanks.'

There weren't words.

Will grinned. '*Sha*.'

All three girls became intensely interested in their soup spoons. Will's chest felt oddly swollen; too big for her body.

'Um . . . I like the soup,' she said. It was a lie: but it was something to say.

'Yes. I mean, *ja*,' said Hannah.

Zoe said, 'Leek, I think . . .'

'Ja. Or potato.'

'Or carrot.'

'It could be anything, really,' said Zoe. 'It tastes like pond water.'

'Ja!' Will grinned. 'Nice pond water, though, ja. Top-quality pond water.'

'Zoe reckons we had cat soup, once.'

'Really?' said Will.

'We did! Seriously, Will. It was definitely cat. There were bits of fur in it.'

'She's making it up, Will. Don't listen to her.'

There was a grumbling, growling noise from

Will's chair. The twins thought it was Will's stomach. They smiled at her, sideways, but said nothing. They were probably too polite to mention it.

Will could feel that it wasn't that. It was the sound of her heart, she thought: it was hope, coughing and stuttering into life.

CHAPTER TWENTY-EIGHT

Will read and re-read Simon's letter in snatched moments throughout the day. It was written on lined paper covered in red dust. She grinned, and rubbed it between her fingers. He must have used the path to the farmhouse as a desk.

'Dear Wildcat,

'I've put in this soil so that you know that all is well. It's farm soil; because I'm still at the farm. Lazarus and Tedias and 8 of the men put together their money to buy it. I don't think they had enough. But the Captain sold it to them anyway. Cynthia almost killed him with a saucepan lid. I don't think he cared.

'I'm keeping a space for you next to my bed in the stables. Nobody's allowed to touch it til you come back.

'I can tell Kezia misses you. Shumba misses you.'

Underneath that line, Simon had drawn a monkey riding a horse. Will's eyes ached with the happiness of it. Neither of them had ever been able to draw horses.

The tail was too long on this one; it looked like it had five legs. Under it, Simon had written,

'But I miss you most.

'Write back soon. I want to know what England is like.

'Simon.'

Will propped up her science textbook so Mrs Boniface wouldn't see what she was writing (they were supposed to be drawing the digestive system. Will was unable to find the digestive system exciting) and tore a page out of her exercise book. Her hand shook with happiness as she tried to write.

'Dear Simon,

'Thank you for writing. I miss you more than I can put on paper.

'England isn't like Africa. There's no dragonflies. But there are some good things.'

That was true. There were girls like the twins. There were books. There was Miss Blake. Will wrote again,

'Daniel is one of the good things. He's coming to visit me this weekend. He's bringing me his comics. You'll like him. When I come back to the farm, I'll try to bring him, and you'll meet. He's almost as tall as you. He can whistle with his fingers, but he can't swim.'

Will bit the end of her pen. She wrote,

'I will come back, Simon. I'll come back to the farm and you. I will, I swear.'

She underlined the last two words in red ink, and drew three stars around them. 'But I have to stay here for a while, my dear. I'm learning how to cartwheel in thunderstorms.

'For now, I'm sending love. All the love I have. Far more than will fit in the envelope, ja. Also –'

The bell went. Will folded up the paper and put it safely in her boot. She would finish it later. But she'd said, more or less, what she had wanted to say.

Letters, Will thought, were like books: they were mostly about love.

Read the first pages of Katherine Rundell's *Rooftoppers* ...

On the morning of its first birthday, a baby was found floating in a cello case in the middle of the English Channel.

It was the only living thing for miles. Just the baby, and some dining-room chairs, and the tip of a ship disappearing into the ocean. There had been music in the dining hall, and it was music so loud and so good that nobody had noticed the water flooding in over the carpet. The violins went on sawing for some time after the screaming had begun. Sometimes the shriek of a passenger would duet with a high C.

The baby was found wrapped for warmth in the musical score of a Beethoven symphony. It had drifted almost a mile from the ship, and was the last to be rescued. The man who lifted it into the rescue boat was a fellow passenger, and a scholar. It is a scholar's job to notice things. He noticed that it was a girl, with hair the colour of lightning, and the smile of a shy person.

Think of night-time with a speaking voice. Or think how moonlight might talk, or think of ink, if ink had vocal chords. Give those things a narrow aristocratic face with hooked eyebrows, and long arms and legs, and that is what the baby saw as she was lifted out of her cello case and up into safety. His name was Charles Maxim, and he determined, as he held her in his large hands – at arm's length, as he would a leaky flowerpot – that he would keep her.

The baby was almost certainly one year old. They knew this because of the red rosette pinned to her front, which read, '1!'

'Or rather,' said Charles Maxim, 'the child is either one year old, or she has come first in a competition. I believe babies are rarely keen participants in competitive sport. Shall we therefore assume it is the former?' The girl held on to his earlobe with a grubby finger and thumb. 'Happy birthday, my child,' he said.